About the Book

The summer cottagers lived on one side of Lake Kinniwabi, near the Manitoba border. On the other side of the lake lived the Ojibway Indians.

Ken Warren had never given much thought to the tribe until he met Paul Onaman, son of the Ojibway chief. As the two boys fish, explore, and talk together, they become fast friends, finding themselves to be much more alike than they'd at first suspected.

Together they work with Moose MacGregor, the forest ranger, and the other men of the community to try to stop a rampaging forest fire. They plan and fight to prevent Empirico, a giant Eastern company, from taking over the land that Paul's people have lived on for centuries, and the two boys try to catch the thieves—rumored to be Indians—who are ransacking the summer cottages around the lake.

No Word for Good-bye is a fast-moving, yet sensitive story which will leave a deep impression on the reader.

No Word for Good-bye

by John Craig

Coward, McCann & Geoghegan, Inc.
New York

To Jake,
an Ojibway, wherever he is

Chapter 1

The first time Ken Warren met Paul Onaman was on an early July morning of the summer when they both became fifteen.

He had been helping his father with the chores of opening the cottage and was resting for a minute on the boathouse steps when a red canoe came around the point from Bradley's Bay. It came silently, the V of its bow waves broadening gently across the glassy water behind it.

There were two paddlers in the canoe.

In the stern, squatting low over the rear thwart and with his legs curled beneath it, was a short, slightly built man. His face, the color of red cedar, was lined and a little ugly. There were deep crow's feet at the corner of the eyes, and the high cheek bones accentuated the hollows below them. Although he paddled like a young man, the slight hunch to his shoulders and the narrowing of the eyes suggested the first erosions of old age. He wore a stained peak cap set low on his forehead, heavy work pants and a faded plaid shirt. In spite of the oppressive heat of the early morning, the shirt was buttoned tightly at neck and wrists.

The other paddler, in the bow, was a boy whom Ken judged to be of about his own age. His face, firm and smooth, appeared almost round. His complexion, too, was brown with a tint of copper, though not yet as dark as the older man's. His broad shoulders and his posture, relaxed though erect, suggested the strength and grace of a natural athlete. In a few years, Ken thought, he will be a big man. His hair was black and cut short. He wore a white T-shirt with *Lake Kinniwabi* stenciled in green letters across the chest, and faded, but clean, blue dungarees. As the canoe glided in towards the dock, the boy rested his paddle across the gunwales, letting the older man navigate the landing.

Ken's father came out of the boathouse and stood beside his son.

"Must be the two Indians I asked Mr. Simpson to send over," he said, "to help us with the dock. The one's no more than a boy—though he looks strong enough."

Ken walked down the dock to meet them.

"Morning," he said, bending to catch the bow of the canoe.

The man in the stern nodded almost imperceptibly. The boy sprang lightly from the canoe and tied the bow line to a ring in the slanting dock. Then he straightened and turned to Ken. He was slightly heavier than Ken, though not quite as tall.

"Mr. Simpson said to come over," he said. "My name's Paul Onaman and this is my father, Jake. He doesn't know much English."

Ken's father shook hands with the two Indians and explained what needed to be done. The cribs of the old dock had been pushed to one side and the timbers twisted by the force of the spring ice, so that the dock would have to be almost completely rebuilt. The older man seemed to follow most of what he was saying through his gestures, but every now and then Paul Onaman added a comment in his own language.

After a few minutes the four of them started to work, stripping off the old boards with a crowbar and piling them beside the boathouse. It was hot there in the sun, and before long the perspiration was running down Ken's face. His father took a rest every now and then, sitting on the boathouse steps in the shade and sometimes smoking a cigarette. A couple of times he offered his package to the older Indian and each time Jake Onaman accepted cigarette and light wordlessly. He did not share David Warren's rest at such times, but continued to work steadily, keeping the cigarette in his mouth until it burned down almost to his lips.

Ken found it strange working with the other three. Sometimes he and his father exchanged comments, and occasionally Paul Onaman said something to the older Indian. But there was little communication between the two pairs of father and son.

Ken was curious about Paul Onaman and his father. He knew that they were Ojibway and that they came from the Indian encampment in the clearing across the lake. The Ojibway had lived across Lake Kinniwabi ever since the Warrens had first built their cottage there when Ken was still a baby. He was used to seeing them around the station and in Ben Simpson's supply store—the short, squat Indian women in their shapeless housedresses; the men in their heavy rubber boots and working clothes; the thin children with their wide, frightened eyes.

He had passed their encampment many times in his canoe. Their clearing was at the far end of the lake, away from the cottages and near the margin of the bay where the pickerel and big northern pike fed on the minnows in the weed beds. The Indian camp was made up of a few pitched tents and fifteen or twenty shacks, small, crudely built structures made of poles, discarded plywood and boards, birch bark and tar paper. In the summer evenings you could see the smoke of many fires rising against the forest at the edge of the clearing.

But, although Ken had seen Ojibway there every summer for many years, this was the first occasion he had ever had to speak to any of them or to study any of them as individuals. Up until then, summers at the lake had been spent within the atmosphere of his own family and the people in the other cottages.

Although most of these cottages had been there for many years, Kinniwabi was still relatively unspoiled and the far end of the lake away from the station remained firmly in the grip of the wilderness. This was because there was still no road into the lake, the only means of access being by train.

The cottages stretched away from the station along either side of the lake for perhaps a mile in each direction. Beyond the last of them the shore of the lake was unbroken wilderness with the single exception of the Ojibway clearing on the north side. The Warren cottage was the farthest one from the station on the south shore, directly opposite the Indian encampment which stood a half mile away across the lake.

Through the morning the two Indians worked almost without pause. The boy seemed stronger than his father, but the older man more than made up for this in his agility and dexterity. His movements, Ken thought, were in many ways as silent and sure as those of a cat.

In the afternoon the heat grew worse. There was not a breath of air to relieve the glaring sun and, although thunderheads built up several times in the west, they did not precipitate a storm, and the oppressiveness increased. By midafternoon Ken was thoroughly fatigued and his father

10

had retired to the cottage. But Jake Onaman and his son continued to work, seemingly unaware of the heat.

Several times Ken tried to start a conversation with the two Indians, but on each occasion drew no more than a grunt from the man and the barest possible response from Paul.

Only once was there a break in the strangely impersonal association between himself and the two Indians. While they were working a big black squirrel climbed onto the peak of the boathouse and thoroughly scolded them. Ken paused for a moment in his work to watch the squirrel, which was sitting up on its hind feet and berating them with all the energy in its tiny body. The sound was so shrill on the still afternoon air and the action of the squirrel so audacious, that Ken found himself smiling in amusement. Just then he happened to glance at Paul Onaman and saw the flicker of an answering smile on the Indian boy's lips. But it was gone in an instant, almost as soon as their eyes met, and Paul resumed the impassive expression worn by his father.

Towards the end of the afternoon it became necessary to go back into the bush to cut some new timbers for the dock. Jake Onaman took charge then, going through the woods from tree to tree without a word until he found a trunk straight and strong enough to satisfy him. Then he would simply grunt and point to the tree he had selected.

If it had been hot by the water, it was unbearable back in the bush where not even the faintest breeze reached them. In the breathless, humid air the mosquitoes swarmed in stubborn persistence, adding their malevolence to the misery of the heat. Ken and Paul would fell a tree designated by Jake Onaman, and then the three of them would set about trimming the branches with their axes.

Sweat ran into Ken's eyes. His hands became scratched and covered with pitch from the pine branches. Blisters rose on his hands where he grasped his axe.

When they had finished trimming a tree, Ken and Paul would hoist it onto their shoulders and carry it through the bush to the dock. Ken was amazed by the ease with which the Indian boy would hoist his end of the trunk onto his shoulder and by the way he walked so easily through the deadfalls and over the rocks towards the light of the lake shimmering through the trees. Ken's own shoulder was soon rubbed raw from the rough pine bark and he had to fight continuously to keep from tripping in the rough bush. He knew it was illogical, but he couldn't help resenting the ease with which the Ojibway boy carried out his share of the work.

By the time they carried the day's last log out of the bush and laid it in front of the boathouse, he was close to exhaustion. His mother's call for dinner was the most welcome sound he could have heard. He didn't know whether or not he would have enough strength left to drag himself up the path to the cottage. As far as he could tell, Paul Onaman and his father were unaffected by the day's labor. Both looked as fresh as when they had stepped from their canoe that morning.

As soon as the call to dinner came from the cottage, the two Indians went to their canoe and left without a word or a backward glance. In a dozen paddle strokes they were around the point and gone from sight.

Ken sat for a moment longer on the boathouse steps, trying to will some strength back into his sagging body. Then, with a sigh, he dragged himself to his feet and began the slow climb up the rise toward the cottage.

He realized that he was very hungry. Fortunately his mother had made a big dinner—roast beef, scalloped potatoes, carrots, salad, raspberry pie. Ken ate his first helping without pause. Then, after refilling his plate, he listened for the first time to the dinner conversation.

". . . don't trust them an inch," his Aunt Marion was saying. "It wouldn't surprise me at all if they didn't even show up tomorrow. But I forgot—I guess you haven't paid them yet, have you?"

"No, I'll probably pay them when the dock's finished," his father answered.

"Then in that case they'll be back," his aunt said, knowingly. "But, once they get their hands on a little money, you can kiss them good-bye."

"Are you talking about the Indians?" Ken asked.

"Of course," said his Aunt Marion. "They're all the same. Work until they get some money for liquor, and then disappear. And I wouldn't leave anything around that they can steal, either."

"Oh, I think you're a little prejudiced," Ken's mother put in. "I think it's wrong to generalize about any people. Some of them may be dishonest and lazy, but not all."

"How can you say that?" his aunt asked. "They're not like other people—they're more like animals. There just isn't any way to figure them out. But you won't make any mistake if you're suspicious of them—that's for sure."

"Oh, I don't know," said Ken. "One thing certain—they know how to work. Neither of them stopped once all day long."

"No, they certainly tired me out," said Ken's father. "I couldn't stay with them at all."

Ken thought about slight, stooped Jake Onaman, throwing the big timbers around. And he remembered Paul Onaman's jaunty, broad shoulders moving easily under the front end of the logs they had carried out of the bush that afternoon. He was aware of a grudging respect for the two Indians. There was something about their simple, matter-of-fact way of going about things. They were so completely unaffected. And he realized that their taciturn, practical manner was not so much strange, but only different. With his city friends there would have been a more or less steady flow of small talk all afternoon, adding up to not much more than background noise.

He thought about the Indian camp across the lake. I wonder, he thought, what Paul and his father had for dinner. Did their food help to revive them, too? Or were they really as tireless and immune to pain as they had seemed?

Chapter 2

Since the following day was Sunday, there was to be no work on the dock. Ken woke fairly early. He could hear his mother already in the kitchen, lighting the wood stove and beginning her preparations for the breakfast. He stretched luxuriously, watching the flickering patterns of sunlight through leaves on the wall of his cottage bedroom.

His left shoulder was still a little stiff and sore, but otherwise sleep had soothed away most of the aches and weariness. The blisters on his hands and the mosquito bites on his shoulders and arms were still there, however.

He spent the morning doing odds and ends around the boathouse, keeping in the shade as much as possible. Then, early in the afternoon, storm clouds began to build up in the west.

"I think we're going to get a dandy," his father said, standing by the screen door of the dining room and looking across the lake. "Look at those thunderheads piling up there."

"Thank goodness," put in his Aunt Marion. "I hope it cools things off. I don't think I could stand much more of this."

Ken went over and stood beside his father. The black mushrooms of the storm clouds looked ominous, but they were moving very slowly up over the sky.

"I think I have time to catch a couple of fish for dinner before the storm breaks," he said. He knew that after a

15

period of oppressive heat such as they had had, the fish often bite well just before a storm. Sometimes, too, he thought wryly, they won't bite at all.

"Do you think you should go out with a storm like that coming up?" his Aunt Marion asked.

"Sure. I'll be careful and get back before it hits."

He was conscious that his aunt was looking reproachfully at his father and shaking her head vigorously in disapproval. But his father didn't comment, and Ken hurried down the path to the boathouse.

Seconds later he had his rod, tackle box and gaff hook in the boat and was heading up the lake towards the storm clouds. He pushed the throttle of the outboard wide open and watched the bow lift slightly as he straightened the boat away toward the weed bed in the big bay at the head of the lake.

This is the time, he thought, when those big northern pike often strike—when the water is dark and sullen under the clouds. There would probably be a wind before the storm struck and that, too, might be to the pikes' liking. A few minutes later he swung the boat around the rocky point at the beginning of the big bay and throttled the motor back to trolling speed. There was a fallen pine protruding far out into the water just around the point and as he passed a wood duck swam out from behind it with her family of young trailing behind her.

Ken took out a double spinner with red and white feathers around the treble hooks and fastened it to the wire leader at the end of his line. He cast the lure well out behind the boat, letting his forward progress strip off a few extra feet of line before he put his thumb on the reel and felt the throbbing pull of the spinners behind him.

16

He had not gone very far on his first run around the bay before he realized that this would probably not be his day to catch fish after all. A glance behind the boat showed him that the storm clouds, which had seemed such a sure threat a few moments before, were beginning to swing away to the north. Seconds later the sun came out again and the lake once more became a sheet of sparkling glass.

All of Ken's experience told him that it was useless to hope for fish under such conditions. He was about to reel in his line and turn for home when he saw another boat at the edge of the weed bed up ahead. It was a worn red canoe, lying almost motionless on the still water. As he approached he saw that the single figure sitting on the middle thwart was Paul Onaman.

On an impulse he swung the bow of the outboard in towards the canoe, reeling in his lure at the same time. When he shut off the motor it seemed suddenly very still and very quiet. At the same time the heat of the sun became even more evident.

The Indian boy didn't look up. He was holding a long pole, perhaps a dozen feet in length, out in front of the canoe. It looked like a sapling or the branch of a tree cut from the bush.

Ken was a little embarrassed at the continuing silence and found himself wishing he had not approached the canoe. He wished that the boy would look up and say something. He considered starting up the outboard and going on, but that somehow seemed silly. Finally, he decided to take the lead.

"Hi," he called. "How's the fishing? Having any luck?"

Paul Onaman kept looking at the end of his homemade fishing rod, which he held low over the weeds. When he spoke at last his voice was almost inaudible.

17

"Some," he said.

I wonder what he can be fishing for in all those weeds, Ken thought. Maybe for sun fish, or perch, or even large minnows. The Indians probably eat a lot of strange things, he thought, and suddenly realized that he hadn't the faintest idea what he meant by that.

"What are you trying to catch?"

There was another pause before Paul answered.

"*Maskinozha*," he said in the same low voice. And then, seeing Ken's puzzlement, he set his pole down across the gunwales and made a gesture with his hands, spreading them wide apart. "*Maskinozha* Old Long Nose," he said. "Pike."

Ken wondered how anyone could hope to catch pike with an outfit like that in the middle of the weeds on such a hot, still day. Overcome with curiosity, he took the paddle and pushed his boat gently over alongside the canoe. When he could see over the gunwales, his eyes grew wide with amazement. On the bare ribs at the bottom of the canoe lay three fat pike, one still twitching violently. That one, the largest, would be well over ten pounds.

"How do you catch fish like that on a day like this?" Ken asked in astonishment.

The Indian boy smiled lightly for the first time.

"Here, look, I'll show you," he said, lifting up his home-made pole.

At the end was tied a piece of stout cord no more than a yard long. There was a large, single hook and on the hook was a big, green frog.

"You mean that's how you caught those pike?" Ken asked incredulously.

"Sure," said Paul Onaman. "Like this." He lifted the long

pole, swung the frog out and dropped it in a small hole between two clumps of weeds. He let it float gently down into the water, left it for a few seconds, then swung it over to another opening in the weed-filled bay.

"On a hot day like this," he said, "Old Long Nose likes to get in the shade of the deep weeds. Do you want to try it?"

Ken took the pole. It felt heavy and awkward after his own light casting rod.

"Wait," Paul said. "Try over there beside those lily pads." He pushed Ken's boat gently a few feet to one side.

"There," he said. "Try there."

Ken swung the frog out over the water and dropped it into the small opening between the lily pads.

"Let it sink gently," Paul said quietly.

Ken really had no faith in what he was doing. He thought of what his Aunt Marion had said and wondered if Paul was making fun of him.

Then suddenly the stout pole jerked sharply in his hands.

"There," said Paul. "Pull it in! Pull it in!"

Ken tried to manipulate the long pole. The fish was much too heavy to swing out of the water.

"Run your hands along the pole towards the end," Paul said.

Ken did this, moving one hand up ahead of the other until he reached the end, and letting the rest of the pole go into the water behind him.

"There, that's it," said Paul. "Now, grab the string."

Ken dropped the rod and caught the short line in his hand. The pike was thrashing and straining against the pull, but, with a sudden heave, he swung it into the boat. It was a good-sized fish—perhaps eight or nine pounds.

19

"Well, I'll be," said Ken. "I wouldn't have believed it in a million years. Do you always fish like that?"

"Sometimes," Paul said, "especially on a hot day like this. Other times you fish in deep water maybe, or on the shoals. It depends."

"Well anyway, there's our dinner," Ken said. "Thanks for letting me try your pole."

"That's okay," Paul said, "but I think we'd better get going now. It looks like that storm is coming back."

Ken glanced back over his shoulder. The black clouds which had temporarily veered away to the north had changed direction again and were coming up fast behind them. They looked even darker and more ominous than before. As he watched, a streak of jagged lightning ripped the western sky and a gust of wind tore at the calm surface of the water.

"I guess we had for sure," he said. "Anyway, thanks again, and I'll see you in the morning."

"Okay. See you," Paul said, pushing his canoe away from the weeds and taking up a quick stroke with the paddle. Ken opened the motor wide and reached the dock just as the storm broke. The wind was lashing the poplars and the first rain fell as he ran up the path to the cottage.

The storm continued throughout the remainder of the afternoon. For a time it was so dark that Ken lit a couple of coal oil lamps so that he could read in his bedroom. But by dinner time the clouds had passed. It was definitely cooler, and the world had a fresh, newly washed smell as Ken went down to the boat with his father to drive him over to catch the train. The Cottager's Special went through Kinniwabi at eight o'clock, reaching the city a little after ten thirty.

20

As they crossed the lake, Ken saw several other boats, all focusing on the station as if it were the hub of a wheel.

When they climbed the short hill from the dock to the station there were several people already there to meet the train. The contrast between the formal city clothes of those who were catching the train and the informal garb of those who were to remain always amused Ken.

"Well, we've got twenty minutes or so," his father said. "Why don't we go over to the store and get the things you need before the train arrives?"

They walked along the station platform, crossed the tracks, and went up the narrow boardwalk to Ben Simpson's store. It was a low wooden building, many years old and in some need of painting. Across the peak of the roof was a long sign, white with faded red letters, which said: KIN-NIWABI STORE; BEN SIMPSON, PROP.

Inside, through the screen door, the store looked ram-shackle and old-fashioned. The linoleum-covered floor un-dulated in random waves. In the center was a galvanized iron stove, obviously chosen for its efficiency rather than its appearance. Several wolf and fox pelts hung beside the door. The shelves contained many fascinating items other than groceries—traps, nails, hatchets, boots, shirts, lanterns, shotgun shells, twine, bolts of cloth, and numerous similarly assorted articles.

Ben Simpson was somewhere in his mid-seventies. He was a tall man, sparse of frame, and stooped now from rheuma-tism or some early injury, or both. One eyelid had become permanently disabled long ago, giving it a fixed, slightly staring appearance. A long, thin nose highlighted his lined face. His still-thick head of hair was parted in the middle

21

and combed straight back on either side. He had first come to Kinniwabi as an R.C.M.P. constable over a half century before and remained there ever since. He made his living from the store and from trading with the Ojibway and Cree in furs and wild rice. Kinniwabi was in the heart of the somewhat limited wild rice belt, and during September Simpson shipped hundreds of bags of it, in years when the crop was good.

He was talking with Moose MacGregor, the forest ranger, when the Warrens came in.

"Did you hear about the robbery?" Mr. Simpson asked, after they had exchanged greetings.

"No," Mr. Warren replied. "What robbery?"

"Somebody broke into Dr. Moir's place last night," said Moose. "They say they stole a camera and a transistor radio and some other things. The Moirs went up to the city for a few days last week. Looks like somebody decided to take advantage of their absence."

"Well, that's too bad," Ken's father said, shaking his head slightly. "We haven't had a robbery around here for a long time. I wonder who could have done it?"

Suddenly a new voice spoke out from the back of the store. It was a low, deep voice, but loud enough that everyone in the store could hear.

"Well, that shouldn't be no mystery, should it, Mr. Warren?" asked the voice. "Most everybody knows who does the stealin' around a place like this. The Indians, that's who done it. Just like always."

Ken turned to see the huge bulk of Wilbur Crowe leaning on a counter in the dim light farthest from the door. He was an immense man, dressed in faded and loose-fitting overalls over a coarse work shirt. A floppy and dirty old fedora was pulled low on his head. There were two figures on a bench nearby—Wilbur's equally big son, Les, and his friend Dinnie Hackett, who seemed to cringe into the shadows.

"How do you know?" asked MacGregor. "How do you know it was the Indians? Nobody's got any proof in any direction as yet. You're just jumping to conclusions."

"Mebbe so," said Wilbur Crowe, putting a newly rolled cigarette into his mouth. "Mebbe so, but I'll tell you this—them Indians that did it had better jump before they get caught."

Dinnie Hackett broke into high-pitched laughter, and Les Crowe smiled with his thick lips, though not, Ken thought, with his eyes.

"It strikes me some people are too quick to make accusations," Moose MacGregor said.

"Are you gonna help us mend our ways?" Les Crowe asked, taking a step toward the front of the store.

But just then they all heard the faint sound of a whistle from somewhere up the track, and there was a sudden movement to gather belongings and get across to the station.

The train whistled again as they stepped onto the platform, much closer this time, and a few moments later they saw the prematurely lit headlight on the front of the big engine swing around the bend. The platform was filled with the sound of the bell and of escaping steam as the engine went by, slowing for the station.

"Well, I'll see you Friday night," Ken's dad said as he swung up the steps.

"Board," the conductor called, putting his watch back in the pocket of his blue vest, picking up the small portable step and swinging up between the cars as the train slowly gathered speed.

Ken waved to his father and a moment later the last coach of the train swung out of sight into the rock cut a half mile down the track. The station seemed strangely silent and empty once the train was gone.

Ken turned with the other people and started down the path toward the boat. As he did so, he noticed Wilbur and Les Crowe and Dinnie Hackett walking slowly along the track in the direction the train had gone. Dinnie Hackett's tinny laughter came to him across the stillness of the evening air and it occurred to Ken that there was no more humor in that laugh than he had seen earlier in Les Crowe's eyes.

Chapter 3

The next day was much cooler. Ken and Paul and Jake Onaman worked at straightening and repairing the cribs which would be the foundation for the rebuilt dock. It was a difficult job. Ken and Paul spent most of the day standing in water that often reached to their shoulders. It was awkward grappling with the heavy stones under the water and both of them skinned their knuckles several times before the day was over. By then Ken was as chilled as he had been overheated two days earlier.

Paul Onaman seemed as impervious to the cold as he had previously been to the heat. Towards the end of the day they began to rebuild the main supports which tied the cribs together and formed the foundation for the board top that they would nail on as the final step.

Paul's father was a true craftsman with an axe. He used a fairly small blade with a short handle and most of the time he swung it with one hand, holding it a few inches below the head. The logs had to be fitted to ensure solid joints and Jake Onaman cut the necessary notches with the sure stroke and precision of a cabinetmaker.

Ken had his lunch that day with the two Ojibways at the boathouse. Something had bothered him about the fact that on Saturday he had had lunch at the cottage while the Indians had eaten at the scene of their work. He had thought about it several times on Sunday, and during the morning he had gone up to the cottage to talk it over with his mother.

"Why don't we ask the two of them up here for lunch?" he asked her as he entered the kitchen.

His mother was mixing a cake.

"Well . . ." she began.

"I should say not," his Aunt Marion broke in. "What on earth are you thinking of, Ken? I wouldn't want them around the cottage. You can't tell what might turn up missing. Besides they wouldn't feel right up here. They have their proper place, and they know it."

"It's pretty cold down there today," Ken said.

"Oh, nonsense," Aunt Marion said. "They practically live outside all winter. They don't feel the cold like we do and anyway, for goodness sakes it's July, not January."

"We could compromise," he suggested. "Suppose I ate my lunch down there with them?"

His mother smiled her thanks, but Aunt Marion was not yet finished.

"That's just plain silly," she said impatiently. "Why eat cold sandwiches when you could come up here and have some good homemade soup?"

"Maybe we can fix that, too," put in his mother. "No reason why I can't give you each a big mug of hot soup to eat with your sandwiches. That should make everybody happy."

While working together there had been little conversation among the three of them. They had exchanged the necessary comments about their work, of course, but beyond that they had worked in silence for the most part. Ken had tried to start a conversation several times, but to little avail. Paul had made no reference that morning to their meeting beside the weed bed at the head of the lake.

He and his father exchanged the occasional comment, always in Ojibway. Ken found the low, nasal sounds difficult to re-create in his mind and therefore hard to remember, but he felt fairly sure now of a few words that had been repeated several times. *Nigouisses*, he felt confident, meant son. *Schiman* was the word for canoe, and *aboui* for paddle. *Notine* was Ojibway for wind. He was most sure of *niguim*. Sometimes when Paul would take a little longer than his father felt was necessary he would be told to *niguim*—hurry up. Just before lunch that day Ken made his first penetration behind the expressionless, lined mask of Jacob Onaman's face. Ken was holding up the end of a timber while he waited for Paul to place a rock underneath it. Paul seemed to be taking his time in finding a rock which suited him.

"*Niguim*," Ken had called, unthinkingly. "*Niguim*, for pete's sake."

A flicker of humor spread across Jacob Onaman's face.

"Yeah, *niguim* . . . *niguim*," he said, and then Paul smiled a little, too.

As they sat on the boathouse steps eating their lunch that Monday, Ken made one or two further attempts to open the conversation, but again neither of the Ojibway responded. Ken did not believe in continuous small talk himself, but he found the relentless silence strange and faintly embarrassing. There did not, however, seem to be a great deal he could do about it.

When they had finished, Jake Onaman took out a pipe, filled it from an oilcloth pouch and lit it. Paul sat looking out across the lake, the water gray under the sullen skies and with whitecaps out beyond the point of the island.

"What do you do in the city?" he asked suddenly. "Do you go to school?"

Ken was taken by surprise. It was the first comment either of the Ojibways had volunteered.

"Yes," he said, "I go to school. Just finished my first year of high school. Grade nine. I'll be going into grade ten in September."

Paul just nodded.

"How about you—do you go to school?"

The Indian boy shook his head, looking down.

"Not any more," he said. "I used to go but I finished a year ago. I stay at home now."

Ken thought of the years of school ahead of him. Four more years of high school and then four years or more of college after that. He tried to think what it would be like to be finished school for good now.

"How come?" he asked. "Don't you go to high school?"

Paul shook his head again, still looking down.

"There is no high school down here," he said.

"Then why don't you go where there is a high school—to the city if you have to?"

Paul's eyes lifted from the ground and turned towards Ken. His look was steady for a long moment, and then he smiled lightly. He did not answer. Instead he spoke a few words to his father. The latter nodded and grunted a one word answer.

"Where did you go to public school?" Ken asked.

Paul pointed towards the station, and told him about the school train. One day a week during the school year the converted railway coach that was their schoolroom sat on the siding at Kinniwabi. Half of the coach had been made into a classroom, complete with blackboard, desks, maps and the other paraphernalia of teaching. Like the historic country schoolroom, it was heated by a coal-burning, pot-bellied stove. The other half of the coach comprised the living quarters of the teacher.

On the day that the school car was at Kinniwabi the children of the district went there and had school much like other children. Then, at the end of the day, the school car would be hitched to some freight train and moved on down the line to spend the next day at another station.

Children of all ages and all grades sat in the same room and the teacher went from one to another of the pupils, dealing with each in turn as well as he could.

"But that was only one day a week," put in Ken. "What about the other four days of the week?"

"The teacher used that day to outline the week's lessons for us," answered Paul, "and we did the rest of the work at home while the school car was away. Then the next week he would review what we had done and give us another week's assignments."

Ken tried to comprehend the kind of teaching Paul described. He could imagine the school car on the siding vividly enough. He thought about what it would be like walking along the track on a January morning with the temperature thirty-five degrees below zero and the wind whipping across the frozen lake. He could picture the frost on the school car windows and the smoke from the chimney curling straight up in the winter air. He could imagine the hot, humid atmosphere of the classroom. But he found that he was unable to grasp what it would be like being left on your own to do a week's lessons at home.

"Do you have any brothers or sisters?" Ken asked.

"Yes, I have a brother, John. He is twenty-two or twenty-three. I forget."

He spoke to his father in Ojibway, the sudden change in pitch and intonation sounding strange to Ken.

"He is twenty-three, my father says. He is working this summer with the forest ranger, Mr. MacGregor. He had T.B. a few years ago, but he is strong now. I had two sisters a long time ago, but they died. I don't know how."

There was another pause.

"Do you have any brothers or sisters?"

"No. I'm the only one. Sometimes I wish I did have, other times I'm glad I'm the only one. I get my way more by being alone."

They exchanged smiles.

"Have your people lived here at Kinniwabi for a long time?" Ken asked.

"They have been here all my life, and a long time before that. The old people tell stories about what it was like here long ago. But I do not really know how long."

He turned again to his father, and spoke at length in Ojibway. When Paul had finished speaking, his father did not answer immediately, but refilled and relit his pipe first. His answer was punctuated with many hand gestures.

"He says that our people have been here since long before the oldest story," Paul translated. "He says that Nanabazho gave this land to our people soon after the world began. We have lived here ever since. The bones of our ancestors—so many that no man could count them—are in the secret place over the high hills to the north."

Ken had a sense of infinite time as he listened to Paul's answer.

"Who is Nanabazho?" Ken asked.

"Nanabazho is what you would call a god or maybe a spirit. He was on the earth long, long ago. He was a friend of my people. He gave us many things and taught us much."

"How long ago did all this happen?"

Paul spoke again to his father. The slightly hunched shoulders shrugged as the answer came.

"My father says that he does not know how long. There is no way to answer because there was no time then. But it was so long ago that no one can truthfully understand it."

Ken looked across the lake at the Ojibway clearing and he thought of the smoke rising from campfires far back in the mists of time. For a fleeting moment he felt a strange sense of identity with all those long-dead people who had once lived here on the shores of Kinniwabi. People who made their fires and killed and ate and slept and lived and died there, centuries before the first white man ventured timidly out into the Atlantic and began to think of a world outside Europe.

Paul's father said something to his son.

Paul smiled. "He says that, however long our people have been here, we have been long enough at lunch. He says it is time to get back to work."

Ken smiled at Jake Onaman and saw a flicker of warmth in the deep-set eyes in return.

At dinner that evening Ken told his mother and his Aunt Marion about the lunchtime conversation. He described the school car and expressed his amazement that Paul had been able to get through public school under the circumstances.

"Wasted," Aunt Marion said. "All that time and trouble and money wasted."

"Why wasted?" Ken's mother asked.

"Well, of course it's wasted. When they do get through grade eight, what on earth good is it going to do them or anybody else? They'll just hang around their village and drink and have all kinds of children and live on what the government hands out to them. We're just building up more expense for the future. And they don't even know enough to be grateful."

"Why should they be grateful, for goodness sake?" asked Ken, his temper rising. "After all they were here long before we were. I don't understand how you can be . . ."

"Now, now, Ken," his mother admonished, "Aunt Marion is entitled to her opinion."

"I suppose so," Ken said, his voice indicating little conviction.

There was a strained silence around the table for several minutes. Ken's mother finally ended it by asking him if he would go over to the station and buy a few groceries that they needed.

The sun was low towards the horizon as Ken cut across the water, around Hewitt's point, and then across the open lake towards the station. The wind was going down with the sun and the lake was completely calm.

As he neared the station a canoe was moving through the shadows close along shore. An old Indian woman sat in the stern paddling with quick, steady strokes. She wore a heavy sweater, many times too large for her, and a faded navy blue tam on her head. A thin girl of ten or eleven years paddled in the bow.

I wonder how many old Ojibway women and young Ojibway girls have paddled how many canoes up this lake, Ken thought? And how many more will there be?

He tied the boat up at the dock and climbed the rise to the station. D. R. Morley, the station agent, was standing on the platform, talking to Wilbur Crowe. The two made a strange contrast. The towering bulk of Wilbur Crowe made the other man seem even more spindly and frail looking. The unkempt appearance of the former made the fastidious neatness of the station agent—white shirt, blue tie, neatly pressed trousers, well-shined black shoes, rimless glasses—seem almost like something from a comic strip.

The two of them were in earnest conversation as Ken approached.

"What I want to know," asked D. R. Morley, "is how many more of them there will be? How long do we have to put up with it? What are the authorities waiting for?"

Wilbur Crowe was smoking a cigar.

"That's the way I think too," he said. "It isn't as if everybody didn't know who's to blame. Lord almighty, there ain't no doubt about it."

"Of course, there's no doubt about it. It makes you wonder what we're paying taxes for . . ."

Ken went on across the tracks to the store.

There he learned that there had been a second robbery. This time somebody had stolen an outboard motor from old Mr. Grimes down in the bay. There were all kinds of rumors circulating. Someone stated it as a fact that an arrest had been made over at Turtle Narrows. Another story claimed that the motor had turned up at Otter Lake. According to this version, two Cree from the Black Dog Reserve were already in custody. Someone had heard that there was some shooting involved in the arrest.

But it was clear that no one had any real facts.

"Talk, talk, talk," Ben Simpson said, shaking his head.

"Everybody talks and nobody knows what they are talking about."

He began to check over the items Ken had selected from the shelves, listing them laboriously with the stub of a pencil. He wrote with a slight quaver now, but the characters retained some of the elegance learned in penmanship classes almost three-quarters of a century ago.

"There's only one thing for sure," he said. "Not much good is likely to come of this. And the more loose talk there is the greater harm there's apt to be."

Chapter 4

Ken pulled his head down still deeper into the collar of his parka as he fought his way into the teeth of the blizzard along the tracks towards the station. His face was stinging and his legs and feet were numb from the cold. The sound of the school car bell came to him spasmodically through the howling winter wind. He knew he was going to be late for class but, try as he might to hurry, he seemed unable to draw nearer to the dim lights of the station up ahead. If only he could lie down and sleep . . .

But he could not sleep. No, no, he must wake up and shut off the alarm before it awakened his mother and Aunt Marion. Having stilled the insistent bell, he snuggled down for another moment under the bed covers and looked at the slanting rays of the early morning sun through his bedroom window. He heard a chipmunk scrambling over the cottage roof and somewhere back in the woods a crow was cawing noisily.

His dream had been so vivid and the cold of winter so authentic, that the transition back to reality was a momentary shock. In spite of the warmth of the morning, he shivered slightly as he sat on the edge of his bed and began to dress. His alarm clock said that it was just past five thirty.

It was a beautiful, still morning. As he walked down the path to the boathouse, the sun was already well above the treetops into a cloudless, brilliantly blue sky. The surface of the lake was dead calm, the reflections stretching out perfectly across the water and making the far shore of the lake seem strangely near.

It's a morning for the canoe, he thought.

He paddled slowly along the shore, gradually working his way towards the head of the lake. A loud slap made him jerk his head to one side and gradually widening circles in the water showed him where a beaver had submerged an instant before. Fish were jumping on all sides. The crow was still keeping up its raucous commentary. How alive it is, he thought—everything is awake and active except for the people sleeping in the cottages. There was as yet no sign of activity in the Indian village.

Ken thought again of his dream and of the incredible contrast between the hostile savagery of the world he had seen in it and the friendly, warm tranquillity of the summer morning. It's funny, he thought, I've been coming here for all these years and felt I knew Kinniwabi so well, and yet I never even really thought of it except as it is between the first of July and Labor Day. Kinniwabi meant summer. During the rest of the year, when he was in the city, the lake had always remained in his mind as it was when he was at the cottage. He had never realized that life, often harsh, went on at Kinniwabi all the rest of the year. That the seasons came and went. That people did their work and went to school and lived their lives there. And that the two smiling months of summer constituted merely an episode, and a largely uncharacteristic episode, in the cycle of those lives.

An hour and a half later when he returned to the cottage, his mother was up and had started a fire in the wood stove in the kitchen. Paul and his father arrived as they were finishing breakfast. The work had gone well and there was a good chance that they would finish the dock that day. All that remained was to cut and nail the planks to form the top surface. It was relatively easy work after the hard labor of the past few days.

At lunchtime Ken and Paul resumed their conversation of the previous day.

"What's it like in high school?" Paul asked.

"It's all right. They say it gets a little harder each year and you have to work more at home all the time. But I like it."

"What do you do besides study?"

Ken told him about his school life. He talked at considerable length, telling Paul about his teachers, his friends, and trying to describe what life was like in the city. He wanted somehow to say how it really was for him. Normally inclined towards reticence, he was surprised at how readily the words flowed.

"I think I'll play football for the school this fall," he said, "but I like hockey best."

"I like hockey, too," Paul said. "We usually keep a rink, clear over on the other side of the island."

Ken looked across the sparkling water and tried to visualize a hockey game in progress there. The vision would not come clearly.

"Once when I had to go to the doctor's at Beaver Lake I saw a hockey game on television," Paul continued. "I saw the Maple Leafs playing against the New York Rangers. You could see it all, right there in the picture. I sure was excited. Did you ever see hockey on television?"

Ken thought about Saturday nights at home in the winter. He and his father always watched the game on TV. They usually put a fire on in the fireplace. They often made popcorn and once in a while his father would send out for a pizza or some Chinese food. They would try to predict the score of each game before the telecast came on, and afterwards they would guess who the three stars would be. He wondered how many games he had seen that way—a hundred? Two hundred?

"Yes," he said, "I've seen it a few times. I like to watch it when I get a chance, but it's not nearly as much fun as playing yourself, is it?"

"You remember yesterday," Paul asked, "when you were asking me how long we had been at Kinniwabi?"

Ken said that he remembered very well.

"I was talking about it last night to my brother, John," Paul said. "He works for Mr. MacGregor, the forest ranger."

"Yes, I remember you told me that."

"Well, he says that we may not be here much longer." He looked down at the ground in front of the boathouse, and Ken sensed that Paul was telling him something that he regarded as important.

"How's that?"

"Well, John doesn't know all the details, but it seems the land where we have our camp belongs to someone else. The story is that whoever owns it is going to make us leave."

"You don't know who owns it?"

"No."

It seemed to Ken a strange thing that in the infinite wilderness around Kinniwabi anyone would feel obliged to exercise the rights of private ownership. He said so to Paul.

"We can't understand it either. We always thought that the land was ours, but John says it was signed away in a treaty a long time ago."

38

"Oh well, it's inconvenient," Ken said, "but does it make any real difference? You can just move the camp somewhere else close by, can't you?"

"That's what I thought at first, too," Paul said slowly, "but I don't think it's that easy. They say we can't use any part of the north shore of the lake and the south shore past where the cottages are is too swampy."

He spoke to his father at some length in Ojibway.

"Actually, it's pretty serious," Paul continued. "We'll have to go quite a bit further north to find any other suitable land that we can use. Here the children can go to the railway school. We're right in the middle of the wild rice belt here, and we can bring the rice in to trade with Mr. Simpson."

He was drawing a rough pattern in the sand with a twig. It was in the shape of a fish.

"We can probably survive somewhere else, all right," he continued, "but it will be much harder. We've been here for so long."

Ken tried to imagine what it would be like if his family and all their neighbors in the city were suddenly told that they had to pack up and leave.

"That's pretty tough," he said slowly, "but maybe something can be worked out."

"It will be bad for the old people, having to go to a new place," Paul said. "They want to die where they have always lived. And it will be bad for the children. Winter in a new place will be hard."

"Isn't there something you can do about it?"

The Indian boy shrugged and looked intently at the sand.

"No, there is nothing we can do except wait until they tell

39

us what to do. Mr. Simpson is finding out what he can for us."

There was silence for a few seconds between them.

"Ah, it doesn't matter," Paul said. "One place is as good as another. It has happened to many other bands of our people. Our turn was sure to come sooner or later."

There was a faint new edge of bitterness to his voice and it was quite clear that it did matter, to Paul and to his people. They fell silent after that and soon went back to work on the dock. By the end of the afternoon the last board had been cut and nailed in place and their work was finished.

Paul and his father gathered up their tools and prepared to leave. Ken paid Mr. Onaman what he said, through Paul, was owing to them. It seemed to Ken to be an extremely small sum for the amount of work they had done, but not knowing what to say about it, he merely handed over the money.

The two Indians got into their canoe and pushed away from the rebuilt dock. Paul picked up his paddle, but before taking the first stroke, he turned back towards Ken.

"Thanks," he said. "Are you going to be here all summer?"

"Yes," Ken said. "We'll be here right 'til Labor Day."

"Maybe you'd like to come over some day," Paul said, looking down at the dock. "We could go fishing together, or take a trip somewhere, or something."

"I'd like that," Ken said. "Let's take a canoe and go down the creek to Scott Lake. There's some really big pike in that lake."

The Indian boy nodded and then, turning away, dug his paddle into the water and the canoe moved rapidly away from the dock.

Ken washed up and then climbed the path to the cottage for dinner. While they were sitting at the table, he told his mother and Aunt Marion what Paul had told him.

"That will be a real hardship for them," his mother said. "I wonder what they'll do?"

"Pass me some more of that salad, please," Aunt Marion put in.

"How could I go about finding out the whole story?" Ken asked. "Who would know what it's really all about?"

"I would think—" his mother began.

"That really is a lovely salad," Aunt Marion interrupted. "That dressing is just out of this world. Did you make it yourself?"

"Yes, I made it. Now, about the Indians, Ken, I would think—"

"I just love the summer when you can get all the fresh vegetables," Aunt Marion broke in again. "It's so nice to have new lettuce and radishes. I can hardly wait until the home-grown tomatoes come in."

Ken's mother looked at her sister with a mixture of exasperation and compassion.

"Now, if you think you've finished about the salad and fresh vegetables, Marion," she said, "perhaps you'll let me answer Ken's question."

"Of course, if you want to go on about that," his aunt said, "then go right ahead. Although what on earth difference it can possibly make, I'm sure I don't know. Whatever the real owners do with the land, you can be sure it will be put to better use than those Indians make of it."

Ken's mother waited for a long moment, looking intently at her sister as if to ensure that she had really finished.

"As I was saying, Ken, Mr. Simpson at the store will

41

probably know more about it than anyone else. He usually acts as a sort of unofficial representative of the Indians."

"I wish there was something we could do about it," Ken said. "It just doesn't seem fair when you look at all the unused land around here that somebody should be able to kick them out."

"I know," said his mother. "You wouldn't think the land was worth much to anybody else, either."

"Well, I'll go over and talk to Mr. Simpson tomorrow," Ken said. "Maybe I can at least find out what it's all about."

"Oh, for heaven's sake," muttered Aunt Marion.

Ken helped himself to another piece of apple pie. Outside the cottage windows the sun was low in the west and across the lake the lights had come on at the station. Ken remembered his strange dream. He recalled again the bitter winter wind, the lights of the station through the swirling snow and the terrible frustration of being unable to reach it. It must, he thought, be a little like that for Paul and his people as they tried to achieve an understanding of the white man's alien laws.

"Well, it certainly can't do any harm to find out about it," said his mother, as she got up to clear the dishes. "The law is the law and there is probably nothing that can be done. But you never know until you try."

Aunt Marion sighed her exasperation.

"If you ask me," she said, haughtily, "you're just wasting your time."

"Well, nobody did ask you, Marion," said Ken's mother, losing her patience at last. "But, since you bring it up, let me suggest that being concerned with justice is never a waste of time. Go ahead, Ken, and more power to you."

Chapter 5

The next day dawned gray and sullen. Low, angry clouds tumbled wildly across the sky, driven by a hostile wind. The treetops dipped violently over the cottage and the wind whined bleakly through the screens. The dark surface of the lake was lashed into whitecaps which broke jaggedly on the rocky point. A cold rain lashed against the windows as they ate breakfast. The temperature had plunged downwards through the night. It was one of those peculiar summer days when October momentarily intrudes on July.

Ken spent the morning reading and doing a few odd chores around the cottage. After lunch the wind appeared to have abated slightly and the occasional patch of blue appeared between the clouds. But the sky still looked bleak and cold and the waves continued to run high as he nosed the outboard away from the dock and turned towards the station.

He had put a big rock in the bow to provide ballast, but the boat still careened erratically in the sullen swells. Every now and then it would be caught in the crest of a wave and the motor would race as the boat was carried rapidly forward. Ken had to fight to keep on course and he knew that he would be drenched by the spray on the way home. But he liked the wild freedom of the wind and waves. He knew that there was no danger as long as the motor kept running. But if it ever stopped, he could be dashed against the far shore and the boat seriously damaged or sunk on the rocks. Too bad his father hadn't bought the new motor yet.

When he reached the station, Ken tied the boat around at the back of the dock away from the wind. His was the only boat there. Everybody else was content to stay home, warm and dry. They don't know what they're missing, he said to himself.

A freight train, its twin engines laboring against the gradual rise to the east, was passing through the station as he climbed the hill from the dock. The ties rose and fell slightly as the freight cars rumbled by beside the station platform. It seemed amazing that the slender rails could withstand the pounding. The incredible mass of the great train impressed him as he waited for it to pass so that he could cross to the store. The engines had long disappeared around the bend to the east before the caboose finally swept by, leaving a strangely flat silence.

A young Indian woman and two small children were sitting on some empty soft drink cases to one side of the store entrance. The woman appeared profoundly weary. The childrens' faces were thin, almost gaunt, and their eyes seemed unnaturally large. They did not appear to be waiting for anyone and Ken found himself wondering why they were sitting there. He couldn't imagine a white woman being there with her children in just that way.

The store itself was empty of customers. Mr. Simpson was refilling some of his shelves with canned goods. A few drops of rain lashed against the front windows as Ken entered, and the light inside the store was dim.

"Guess it's time to light a lamp," Mr. Simpson said, moving towards the front of the store. "It seems funny in the middle of a July afternoon, but I swear today seems more like late fall than midsummer."

He lit two coal oil lamps, replacing the chimneys when he had turned the wick to a height that suited him.

Mrs. Simpson came to the door at the back of the store leading into their living quarters. She was a small, neat woman, white haired and wrinkled, but with a vivaciousness in her eyes which belied her years.

"You picked a bad day to come out," she said to Ken. "My lands, it's cool enough to send everybody back to the city."

"Yes, it feels as if it might snow," Ken said. "Actually we do need a few things, but the main reason I came over was that I wanted to talk to Mr. Simpson."

"Well, it's a good day for talk, Ken," the old storekeeper said. "Not much good for anything else, though, except sleeping."

He put the two coal oil lamps up on a ledge over the main counter.

"Let's go in the living room if we're going to talk," he said. "There won't likely be any customers today anyway and if anybody does come in, I can hear them."

The Simpson's living room was pleasant and bright with just a slight touch of the old-fashioned about it. A sturdy couch with a wool afghan over its back dominated one wall, counterbalanced by a majestic grandfather's clock on the wall opposite. On top of a huge upright piano were stuffed and mounted figures of a black duck, a partridge, a young fox and an owl—relics of a period when Mr. Simpson had exercised an interest in taxidermy.

"Well, Ken, what's on your mind?" asked Mr. Simpson when they had taken seats.

45

Ken told him about his conversation with Paul. The old man listened carefully, interrupting him once or twice to ask a question.

"It seems like a really tough break," Ken concluded, "and I was wondering if you could tell me any more about it."

"There isn't much more to tell," Mr. Simpson said. "It appears that the land belongs to a company called Empirico. It's a subsidiary of some giant corporation down east."

Mrs. Simpson brought in a tray with tea, a glass of milk for Ken and a plate of cookies. Mr. Simpson added cream and sugar, stirred, and sipped at his cup before he continued.

"It's hard to get any clear details. We've had several letters from lawyers, but they don't say much outside of the fact that the Ojibway have to go. They're really not much more than form letters."

"Have you tried the government authorities?"

"Yes, I've written to them, but they don't appear to know any more than we do. They seem disposed to feel that the company has a case, though. I guess they probably have, too."

The old man's usually vibrant voice was low and dispirited and there was a tinge of despondency in it. In the sixty years he had been at Kinniwabi he had fought on the Indians' behalf a great many times. Why, thought Ken, he's had this store for almost half a century. Once, many years ago, there had been two stores at Kinniwabi—Ben Simpson's and another run by Wilbur Crowe. But Crowe's sullen disposition, his drunkenness, and a tendency to hand out light weights and heavy bills had forced him out of business.

"I've seen it happen too often to hold out much hope for the Indians," Mr. Simpson continued. "Over the years the bands in these parts have been forced father back into the wilderness one by one. Jake Onaman's band here at Kinniwabi is about the only one left along the railway line now."

He paused for a moment to light his pipe.

"About the time I first came here they were still almost entirely self-sufficient. Even now they are pretty independent and in many ways live as they always have lived. We haven't done much for them, but we've done just enough to make them vulnerable."

"It would be very hard on the old people," Mrs. Simpson put in. Ken remembered that Paul had said the same thing.

"And on the children," he added.

The two old people nodded.

"There's the wild rice, too," said Mr. Simpson. "It grows north of here, too, of course, but Kinniwabi's by far the best base from which to work during the rice season."

He smoked his pipe thoughtfully for a long moment.

"Why, Jake Onaman has come down McGuire's Creek many times with his canoe loaded right up to the gunwales with rice. He and his people are just beginning to build up a little economic stability with the rice and some hard trapping in the winters. He's a good leader and his people are an industrious lot."

"And now they're going to lose it all," Mrs. Simpson said quietly.

"I wish something could be done about it," Ken said.

"It just doesn't seem right. What does the company want the land for, anyway?"

47

"That's one of the things we haven't been able to find out. Maybe for no reason at all. Maybe they just discovered in their records that it belongs to them and they want to put signs on it and keep other people off it."

"Why don't you ask your dad about it?" Mrs. Simpson asked. "He's a businessman and he might know how to find out more details."

Ken had already made up his mind to do that when his father returned on the Friday night train for the weekend. He thanked the Simpsons for the tea, picked up the groceries his mother had asked for and went down to the boat.

The waves were still running high as he headed towards the point. The bow plunged and bucked, and spray came back on him in an almost continual shower. He was thoroughly soaked by the time he reached the cottage and the wind had chilled him through. He had a brisk rubdown and changed his clothes before dinner. Afterwards he lit a bright fire in the fireplace against the chill of the evening.

When he went to bed the wind was still blowing at near-gale force. The branch of a pine tree rubbed violently against a corner of the cottage. Ken snuggled happily under his warm eiderdown and quickly fell into a deep sleep.

At first he didn't know what had awakened him when he returned to consciousness a couple of hours later. The first thing he realized was that the wind had stopped. The black night outside his bedroom window was completely still. From somewhere far away came the monotonous, lonely cry of a whippoorwill.

He lay there, wondering why he had wakened and thinking over his conversation with Mr. Simpson. The proposed eviction of the Ojibway bothered him a good deal and he had determined to get to the bottom of it if at all possible. There was probably nothing he could do to change the situation, but at least he might be able to learn the basis of its inevitability.

But that could keep until tomorrow, when his father arrived on the train. There wasn't much he could do about it now, in the middle of the night. He rolled over, pulled the covers up tight under his chin and closed his eyes. He had begun to drift off once more when a faint noise drew his attention.

What was that?

He sat up in bed, listening carefully. For a moment he heard nothing except the whippoorwill. Probably his imagination, he thought. But wait, there it was again—a faint scraping sound. He should know that sound. Ah yes, that was it—a paddle scraping lightly against the gunwale of a canoe.

Someone was paddling past the cottage, close inshore by the point. What on earth would anyone be doing out in pitch darkness in the middle of the night?

He listened intently. The faint sound had an eerie quality to it. In the still night it almost seemed to be in the bedroom with him. The sound was moving gradually from west to east.

And then he heard the voice. It was little more than a whisper, scarcely more audible than the faint scrape of the paddle. He couldn't make out what had been said. There was another vague sound which might have been someone else grunting in answer. Then he heard the first voice again.

Ken went quietly over to the window but could see nothing in the blackness, not even the outline of a tree.

He didn't hear the voice again, and in a moment the sound of the paddle scraping was gone into the darkness. Standing there by the window he could almost believe that he had imagined the whole thing—almost but not quite. He could still hear that faint voice in his mind. Barely audible though it had been, it seemed to Ken that there was something vaguely familiar about it.

He might have thought it was a couple of Indians out catching bullfrogs by flashlight, except that the rhythm of the speech seemed somehow more English than Ojibway. And, even though the voice had been little more than a whisper, there had been a high pitch to it that eliminated the possibility of it having been Indian in origin.

Ken lay in bed in the darkness and tried to put his finger on the reason for the voice's elusive familiarity. He had heard that tinny voice within the past few days, he was sure. Where had he heard it? Whose voice was it? He didn't know why it was so important, but he wanted desperately to make an identification.

Think, think, think, he said to himself. But inspiration didn't come and after a while Ken's eyes gradually closed and he drifted back to sleep.

The last embers in the fireplace crackled once and the whippoorwill continued its lonely chorus back on the ridge behind the Warren's cottage.

Otherwise all was silent in the black night.

Chapter 6

For Ken there was always something special about Fridays at the lake. There was, of course, the basic fact of his father's arrival on the evening train. Ken was fond of his father and liked having him around. He was old enough now to take a fairly objective view and he had come to the conclusion that his father was, as the thought existed in his own mind, a pretty good guy.

It was always interesting, too, to hear the news from the city, news of their neighbors and friends. And his father always brought down some new reading material, as well as fresh meat and other things that they couldn't get at Ben Simpson's store.

There was also the fact that he more or less *had* to meet the train on Friday evenings, come rain or shine, wind or storm. Literally, of course, this was not quite true. If the weather was completely hopeless, his father could wait at the station with the other weekenders until it cleared sufficiently for boats to get over from the cottages. But, short of something like a hurricane, custom dictated that the weekend train would be met, even if it meant going out in weather that would otherwise keep the boats tied securely to the docks at home. And Ken liked the adventure implied by this custom. He recognized this as naïve and could smile at it to himself, but he was honest enough to admit that, nevertheless, he enjoyed it.

This particular Friday there were several special reasons

for anticipation. He was hoping that his father would bring down the new outboard motor they had talked about buying. Then, too, the next day was Ken's birthday and he was excited about the gifts his father would probably have been commissioned to pick up in the city. And, finally, he was impatient to talk to his father about the plight of the Ojibway.

As he neared the station dock that evening he saw a familiar figure standing near a red canoe. It was Paul Onaman. He was tossing pebbles over towards the weed bed beside the dock. He gave no sign of having seen or recognized Ken as Ken cut the motor and the boat drifted gently in to the side of the dock. Ken jumped out and, as he tied up the bow rope, looked up at Paul who was still staring out over the water.

"Hi, Paul," Ken said. "What's new?"

The Indian boy tossed another stone out into the lake.

"Not much," he said.

"I figured it was you as soon as I noticed the red canoe," Ken said. "It's the only one like it on the lake."

Paul made a stone skip across the surface.

"Are you going up to the store?" Ken asked.

The Indian boy did not answer. He walked along the edge of the dock, dropping his remaining stones one by one into the water. A sunfish came up out of the weeds and looked curiously at one of the pebbles as it drifted gently downward. The fish pushed at it with its mouth, then drifted down again towards the sandy bottom. Paul sat on the edge of the dock, his feet in the red canoe.

Ken looked at his back, not understanding the boy's silence, and was about to shrug and go on up to the store when Paul spoke in a low voice.

"You didn't come over," he said.

There was something intense in the boy's voice that made Ken hesitate before he answered.

"Well, I haven't yet," Ken said, "but I'm going to soon. The weather has been terrible and there have been a few things I had to do."

"How about going fishing tomorrow?" Paul asked. "You could come over early and we could portage into Duck Lake."

"I don't think I can tomorrow," Ken said. "It's my birthday and my parents will want me to stick around. I'll tell you what, let's make it Sunday. I'll come over in the morning. Okay?"

Paul still did not look at him, but he continued to stare intently at the bottom of the canoe.

"We'll see," he said. Then he looked up at Ken for the first time. "Okay, Sunday. If you come."

Ken went on up toward the store. There were still about twenty minutes to train time, but already the station platform was crowded. People were standing in little groups, talking. Children were repeatedly called back, or hauled back, from the edge of the platform in deference to the awaited train which was still a.dozen miles down the track. Probably, thought Ken, about Malatoba.

At the far end of the platform near the door to the station, Ken saw John Onaman, Paul's older brother, talking to Janet Morley. Apart from the fact that he was taller and considerably heavier, John looked a good deal like Paul. He had the same black hair, the same nose and the same soft eyes. Janet Morley, the station agent's daughter, was an attractive brown-haired girl of twenty-one, two years younger than John. She had spent most of her life around Kinniwabi and had gone to the school train, as had John and Paul. Now, she was a university student in the city, returning to Kinniwabi only for the summer months. Their dress presented a strange contrast—Janet, in white shorts and a bright orange blouse, was barefooted; John wore heavy work trousers, a faded khaki shirt and lumber boots laced up to the knees.

They were talking and laughing lightly, but as Ken approached, D. R. Morley came out of the station door. He was impeccably dressed as always and even the green eye-shade he wore on his forehead could not detract from his neat appearance. He held a paper in his hand—probably train orders, Ken thought. There was an angry look in his eyes.

"Janet," he said in a carefully controlled voice, "would you please go in and help your mother now."

"Okay, Dad," the girl said, "as soon as I hear the end of John's story. I'll only be a second."

The station agent stood looking at them for a long moment.

"No," he said finally, "not in a second. I mean now."

The two young people turned their heads to look at him.

"And, as for you," he said to John in an icy voice, "do me a favor and get off this platform. And be quick about it."

Janet Morley looked at her father with shock in her eyes. She seemed to be seeking some sign that he was joking.

"Dad," she began hesitantly, "what's wrong? Why does John have—"

"Never mind why," her father said, his voice rising, "just let him get out of here right now. That's all. I don't want any thieving Indians around you."

The cottagers along the platform were looking in their

direction, curiosity and surprise showing in their eyes. From the back of the platform came a high-pitched snicker. Glancing in that direction, Ken saw Les Crowe and Dinnie Hackett, amused looks on their faces, sitting on a baggage truck. It was Dinnie Hackett who had laughed. Otherwise there was a stunned silence.

John Onaman looked into Mr. Morley's eyes for a long moment and then, wordlessly, turned and walked off the platform towards the dock. Janet Morley, with tears in her eyes, stood looking at her father.

Then she spun on her bare heel and went into the station. Her father took one challenging look along the length of the platform and followed her through the door. The various groups of people returned to their own conversations and Ken turned to cross the tracks to the store.

The first person he saw inside was Moose MacGregor. "One thing I don't understand," the forest ranger was saying, "is what Morley meant by that crack about thieving Indians. Do you think he meant that John has something to do with these robberies?"

"Well, if he does, he's dead wrong," Ben Simpson put in. "I'd stake my life on John's honesty."

"Well, I don't want to accuse anybody," a lady customer said, "but obviously somebody is responsible for them. And I'm quite sure it isn't any of the cottagers. Who does that leave besides the Indians?"

"I don't know," Moose MacGregor said, "but I agree with Mr. Simpson. John works with me, you know, and I'm sure as can be that he's honest. Even if it is some of the Indians, I'm certain that John had no part in it."

"Did you hear that there was another robbery last night?" Mrs. Simpson asked Ken. "The Roberts, over by Eagle

Point, lost a brand-new pair of oars and a set of tools from their boathouse. Somebody broke in there last night while they were sleeping."

Ken turned his mind from the conversation around him. He was remembering the incident of the previous night when he had wakened to the sound of a paddle scraping against the gunwale of a canoe. He heard again the strangely high-pitched whisper in the black night. Could it have had anything to do with the robbery? The vague but intriguing familiarity of that voice came to him again. Where had he heard it before? Whose voice was it? Identification was so tantalizingly close, but, try as he would to force his mind, he couldn't quite reach it.

He considered telling Moose about it, but the details were so nebulous that it seemed pointless. What was there to say? Merely that he had heard something in the night—the sound of a paddle scraping and a high-pitched whisper which was vaguely familiar but still unidentified. If the name that belonged to that voice ever came to his mind, then it would be time enough to tell Moose. For the moment he might as well keep it to himself.

The big clock behind the counter told him that the train was due in four or five minutes. He gathered together his groceries and went up to the boardwalk and across the tracks to the station. As he reached the platform, he heard the train whistle for the rock cut around the far end of the lake. Well, wonder of wonders, the Special was on time! Ken could see the light smoke from the diesel engines over the scrub trees by Wilbur Crowe's shack. A moment later the train was slowing to a stop beside the station platform. Almost before it had stopped, the conductor and trainman had jumped down with their portable steps and the Kinniwabi passengers were disembarking. They looked strange and uncomfortable in their city clothes.

Ken saw his father walking towards him from well up the track. He moved along with the others who were going to meet friends and relatives.

"Hi, Dad," he greeted his father. "Can I carry something?"

"Hello, Ken. No, I think I'm all right. Nothing very heavy in the suitcase this time. How is everybody?"

Ken told him that they were fine and that the dock was finished.

"How did it turn out?" his father asked. "Did you and the Onamans do a good job?"

"Yes, I think you'll be pleased," Ken said. "By the way, did you happen to buy the new motor?"

"By the way, as a matter of fact, I did," said his father. "It's in a crate in the baggage car."

Ken was impatient to tell his father about the problem Paul Onaman and the Ojibway were facing, but there was no time to bring it up then. They went down to the boat and crossed the lake to the cottage—one of the spokes of a wheel that was this time radiating out from the station. The sun was touching the treetops in the west now and a light evening breeze had come up.

After dinner, Ken told his father the story as it had been told him by Paul Onaman, plus the few extra details he had learned from Mr. Simpson. As he talked, he realized that it added up to an extremely sketchy story, beyond the bare fact that the Ojibway were about to be evicted from their land.

His father listened with interest, interrupting occasionally to ask a question.

"I don't know why Ken is so worked up about it," Aunt Marion said. "They're a shiftless bunch, anyway—always on the move—and I don't for the life of me see how one more change of scene can possibly matter to them."

"No, I can see that it could be fairly serious for them," Mr. Warren said. "They can build up pretty deep roots, just like anyone else. And Mr. Simpson is a valuable friend for them to have here. But I don't see that there is much anyone can do about it. It's pretty much the government's business, isn't it Ken?"

"Well, one thing is for sure," said Aunt Marion, "and that is that it's none of our business."

"Maybe everyone just says that it's someone else's business," Ken said. "Maybe everyone just shuts their eyes. That way nobody sees any evil—except the Indians of course."

Mr. Warren looked at his son for a long moment.

"Well, there is something in that," he said. "It's easy to say leave it to Charlie. But it sounds like a pretty complicated question for ordinary people like us to tackle. I imagine that the authorities will see that the right thing is done all around."

Ken was far from satisfied with that answer. He was just a little disappointed with his father. He didn't know what he had expected, but his father's response had somehow fallen a little short of what he had hoped for in looking forward to this talk. He knew that there was little to be gained by pursuing the matter further that night.

With an attempt to mask his disappointment, an attempt which he felt was not quite successful, Ken left the living room and went quietly off to bed.

Chapter 7

Most summer cottagers develop a number of special events which become part of an annual program and are done every summer almost as ritual—a trip down this creek, a picnic on that point, a walk along some trail, picking blueberries on a certain ridge.

The Warrens were no exception, and one of the annual rites of their summer was a trip into Lake of the Clouds. This involved taking the boat to the head of the lake and then a walk of some three miles along a twisting trail over a series of rock ridges. This particular summer it was decided to make the trip on Ken's birthday.

Ken and his father went over to the station early in the morning and picked up the new motor. The station agent made no reference to his scene with John Onaman and was, in fact, as affable as he was efficient in completing arrangements for turning over the motor. By ten o'clock Ken and his father had it back at the cottage, on the boat, and adjusted to their satisfaction. By that time the food was ready for the picnic, and soon afterwards they were pulling the boat up at the beginning of the trail into Lake of the Clouds.

The sky was clear and the sun hot, but a brisk west wind kept them from being uncomfortable as they picked their way along the rugged trail. Winding over the rocks and between patches of sumach, scrawny birches and raspberry bushes, the path rose gradually but steadily along its entire length.

At the end of the trail there was a perfect picnic spot in the shade of some towering pines. A small bay there, with a white sand bottom, was so clean and so geometrically rectangular that it seemed almost like a man-made swimming pool. They had a swim and then lunch. Afterwards, while the others settled back in the shade to rest, Ken set off along the shore to explore the far end of the lake. He ambled along, taking his time, stopping to throw a few stones here, pausing to study a beaver lodge there, eating an occasional handful of raspberries.

Well, he thought, I don't feel particularly different today being fifteen than I did yesterday when I was still just a kid of fourteen. I wonder when Paul has his fifteenth birthday? In some ways the Indian boy already seemed considerably older than Ken; in others as naïve as a much younger child.

He worked his way around the shoreline to a flat, rocky point at the far end of the little lake. There he sat down in a hollow in the rock, under the partial shade of a twisted cedar. He pondered the question of what presents might be forthcoming for his birthday. The combination of good lunch and warm sun made him drowsy and he leaned back, relaxed and content. His fingers idly picked up a handful of small pebbles and he began to toss them, one by one, into the clear water of the lake.

One of the pebbles felt sharp and jagged and when he inspected it he saw that it was thin, gray and very hard. Why, that looked like flint. His eyes swept the ground beside him until they found another piece of the same material, and another, and another. There was a whole layer of them over there. And down farther, between those big rocks, there was actually a pile of the same gray chips a foot or more in depth. That was strange. Ken pulled himself to his feet and went over for a closer look. Taking a handful, he let them trickle through his fingers. They were chips of flint and, as he inspected them more carefully, he could see that some of them were fluted in more or less regular patterns along their edges. It was obvious that this had been done by the hand of man and Ken knew that he had stumbled on a place where the Indians had long ago made their arrowheads and other flint tools and weapons. The pile of chips had been left by some unknown craftsmen of long ago, much as a carpenter leaves behind a pile of wood shavings.

Well, he thought, if that is the case it must mean that the Indians spent a good deal of time here at some point in the distant past. Perhaps there would be other evidences of their presence. Let's see now, he thought, if they came here by boat, where would they probably land? They would be using birchbark canoes so they would be looking for some fairly gentle slope of rock which would not tear holes in the bottoms. Over there, on the other side of the point by that pebbly beach, that's where I'd land, he thought. He stood on the shore, staring intently through the clear water at the gradually shelving bottom. This is ridiculous, he said to himself. What on earth do I expect to find?

He had begun to turn away when an unusual shape in the water caught his eye. What was that? There on the bottom, larger than the multicolored pebbles, was a gently curving, beige object. Ken felt a flurry of excitement as he waded out into the shallow water. Reaching down, his fingers came in contact with a smooth surface which did not feel like stone.

61

A moment later he was inspecting what was unmistakably the bowl of a pipe. Made of clay, it was decorated with a series of linear designs and small dots. The decorations looked as though they might have been made with a pointed stick while the clay was still wet. The pipe was in perfect condition.

Ken walked back up the rock and sat again in the shade. His initial excitement was now giving way to a feeling of curiosity and wonderment. How long had that pipe rested there in the shallow water? Who had made it? What had the man been like who had smoked it? He felt a strange sense of identity with that unknown Indian of long ago, as though there were some kind of personal connection between its original owner and himself. Perhaps no other hand had touched it in the interim. It occurred to Ken that the pipe had probably belonged to an ancestor of Paul's, who might have lived there many centuries before the first white man discovered the shores of Lake of the Clouds. There in the bright summer sunlight, on his fifteenth birthday, Ken had an overpowering sense of the timelessness of human existence. He sat looking at the pipe for a long time, pausing occasionally to stare over the sparkling water of the lake, and the trees and hills beyond.

Then he hurried back to the picnic site to show his find to his family. They shared his excitement—with the exception, that is, of Aunt Marion—though the mysteriously intimate sense of association with the original owner did not touch his mother and father as it had previously touched Ken.

"We'll have to be sure and tell the museum people about this," his father said, as they walked back out along the trail. "They'll want to have a record of it and perhaps they'll send someone out to investigate."

It was late afternoon by the time they got back to the cottage. Ken had a swim while his mother and Aunt Marion were making preparations for dinner. The pipe bowl was given a place of honor on the mantlepiece until Mr. Warren could take it into the city and turn it over to the museum. Ken's eyes kept returning to it. The discovery of the artifact had moved him profoundly and the almost mystical sense of the continuity between past, present and future remained strong.

At dinner that night there was no mention of the fact that this was a special occasion. Ken, fulfilling his part in the game, pretended not to notice that the menu included all the things that he particularly liked. Then, after a slight pause following the completion of the main course, his mother came through the door from the kitchen carrying a huge birthday cake with fifteen lighted candles. The three adults sang "Happy Birthday to You," and Ken smiled happily. Yet, strangely, even at that moment he found himself wondering if Paul had ever had a birthday celebration or had ever received birthday gifts. I wonder, he thought, if he has ever received any kind of gift in his whole life?

It was growing dark by now and his father lit two of the coal oil lamps. Then, while they were still sitting around the table, they gave him his birthday presents. The first was an oblong box from his father, the contents of which Ken was completely unable to guess.

When he had torn away the paper he found inside a camera with adjustable lens and a flashbulb attachment. He had never tried his hand at photography, but the prospect intrigued and pleased him. He glanced briefly through the instruction booklet and looked forward to studying it in more detail at his leisure. He thanked his father and then set about opening another, larger box which his mother handed to him.

His pleasure was intensified on finding that the second package contained a complete outfit for developing and printing photographs—developing trays, developing fluid, fixer, contact printer, negative paper and all the other necessary equipment, with a detailed set of instructions. He put aside the temptation to begin studying the instructions then and there, thanked his mother, and accepted still another package—this time from Aunt Marion. His final gift was a half dozen rolls of film, three in black and white and three for making colored prints.

He was genuinely pleased by his gifts and found no difficulty in conveying his enthusiasm. They sat around the table for a few minutes longer, talking of the day's events. Afterwards, while the two women did the dishes, Ken spread his photography equipment out on the table and began to study it in detail.

After a while his attention wandered and his eyes returned again to the pipe bowl on the mantle. He found himself thinking of the mound of flint chips on the shore of the Lake of the Clouds, of the Ojibway clearing across the lake from the cottage and, inevitably, of Paul. That chain of thought brought him once more to the problem of the pending eviction of the Indians. Then the warmth of the occasion seemed to dissipate, leaving him with a feeling of emptiness. He tried to push it from his mind by forcing his attention back to his newly acquired gifts, but it was no use. The vague feeling of melancholy persisted.

"Guess I might as well turn in," he said, moving towards the bedroom.

"Are you sure you're okay, son?" his father asked. "You didn't get too much sun or something like that, did you?"

"No, no," Ken reassured him, "I feel fine. Just tired, I guess. Thanks a million for everything, Dad, and will you thank Mom and Aunt Marion for me, too?"

He didn't bother to light a lamp in his bedroom, but undressed quickly and got under the covers in the dark. He wasn't really tired and sleep seemed far away. He lay there quietly, looking at the pattern on the ceiling made by the light which came over the partition from the living room.

After a few minutes his father suddenly appeared at the bedroom door and sat on the edge of his bed.

"Okay, son," he said in a low voice, "suppose you tell me what it is that's bothering you."

Ken looked at the ceiling for a further long moment. He was not sure that he could put his thoughts into words.

"Well, all right," he said, "I might as well tell you. I can't get the Indians out of my mind. It seems so unfair that they have to move. And hardly anybody seems to care. Knowing about it seems to take the edge off things."

His father didn't answer immediately.

"This boy is beginning to mean quite a lot to you, isn't he?"

"Well, yes, I like Paul a lot. I don't really know him well yet, but there's something about him that I like very much. It isn't just that, though. It's the whole group of Ojibway that I'm most concerned about."

His father raised one hand and rubbed his forehead.

"It obviously means more to you than I realized," he said after a pause. "I'll have to admit that you're right. It's easy to say you're sorry but point out that it's really not any of your business."

"But somebody has to make it their business—" Ken began.

"No, I know that's right. I'm not arguing with you. It is true that no man is an island, or at least that no man should be."

Neither of them spoke for several seconds.

"Let me think about it," Mr. Warren said at last. "I don't know much about this kind of thing. But give me till tomorrow to mull it over and maybe we can figure out some way at least to make a start."

Chapter 8

Next morning Ken woke early. He had a swim and then, since the rest of the family was not yet stirring, made his own breakfast. He was looking forward to spending the whole day with Paul, yet felt some apprehension. Paul was different in many ways and, though there was already a basis for a deep mutual friendship, Ken knew that both of them would need patience and understanding if it were to have a chance of reaching full development.

After he had eaten, he loaded his fishing gear, bathing suit and a couple of soft drinks into the canoe and started across the lake. It was a perfect morning. The sky was cloudless and the gentlest of breezes made the surface of the lake dance lightly in the bright sunlight. It would be hot later, but not humid.

He paddled easily, enjoying the morning and loving as always the quick response of the canoe under the touch of his paddle. A dog barked from one of the cottages over near the station and the happy shouts of children enjoying a pre-breakfast swim rang clearly through the still air.

The bow of the canoe ground on mud and Ken walked forward, hands on the gunwales to keep the craft steady. He tied the rope around the branch of a fallen poplar tree, pulled the bow up another foot for safety and turned towards the Indian village. The clearing, of irregular shape, was probably a little over one hundred yards wide and slightly more than that in depth. Smoke rose languidly from a half dozen campfires. He could see people moving around the camp, but the only attention paid him was by several dogs who stood at the edge of the buildings and barked loudly. The dogs had the furtive, wary look of foxes or wolves; as if they regarded the whole world as hostile, Ken thought. Their shaggy coats and jauntily tilted ears made them look mischievous and playful, but their staring eyes and tensed, heavy shoulders suggested that they might just as likely attack—and attack to kill.

Ken did not quite know what to do. As he surveyed the camp he could see people of all ages. An old woman tended a fire in the foreground. Two young men stood smoking and talking a little to the left. A group of several small children were playing between the shacks, laughing and shouting as they chased one another. No one so much as glanced Ken's way, though it was impossible for them not to know he was there.

For a long moment he considered the advisability of getting back into his canoe and going home. A strong though intangible wall seemed to turn him away from the encampment. He did not know whether the wall was composed of hostility, distrust, indifference or subservience. Whatever its composition, it was so powerful as to be almost physical in nature.

Perhaps I should forget the whole business and just leave, he thought. But in the instant of conceiving this possibility, he simultaneously rejected it. No sir, he said to himself, Paul asked me to come and I'll be hanged if I'm going to run away from it.

He walked resolutely towards the encampment. Still no single eye was turned in his direction. He selected the two young men, smoking and talking beside one of the nearer buildings.

"Good morning," he said as he drew near them. "I'm looking for Paul Onaman. Do you know if he's around this morning?"

The two men looked at him, then at each other.

"No, don't know," one of them said.

"Paul Onaman," Ken said. "He lives here, doesn't he?"

He realized that his voice was unusually loud. He had raised it in an unconscious belief that increased volume would make what he said more understandable.

"Don't know," said the other man. "Maybe he does. Ask the old woman."

Ken felt frustration. Obviously the man must know Paul. But he did not show his feelings. Thanking them, he turned to the old woman who was nursing the flame of her fire with some dry cedar branches.

"I'm looking for Paul Onaman," he said.

The woman made some unintelligible sounds. Her lips, in the withered parchment of her face, seemed unnaturally fluid over her toothless gums. Her hands, twisted with age, made excited gestures as she talked. It was apparent that she knew no English.

Ken walked over to the children. They stopped their game as he approached and in their wide eyes there was something of the same wariness he had seen in the dogs. They stood watching him, unmoving.

"Hi," Ken said. "Do you know Paul? Where's Paul Onaman?"

The children looked at each other and giggled. A boy of about eight years pushed a slightly younger girl, sending her sprawling onto the tall grass.

"Can you help me?" Ken asked. "I want to talk to Paul Onaman."

Then another boy pointed towards the back of the camp. He was a small boy, with a cap many times too large.

"There," he said. "Maybe Paul is there."

Ken walked in that direction. He felt hot and weary and, in an undefined way, slightly frightened. A halfdozen of the dogs had closed in a tightening circle behind him. Then he saw Paul.

He was sitting on a fallen pine tree and he was alone. He had on the same clothes he had been wearing the first time Ken had ever seen him. As Ken walked towards him, the Indian boy looked up.

"Hi, Paul," Ken greeted him. "What's new?"

A smile flickered at the corners of Paul's mouth.

"Hi," he said. "I was afraid you might not come."

They talked for several minutes about nothing of any consequence.

"Come on," said Paul after a while, "and I'll show you my house."

The shack where the Onamans lived had two rooms. The larger room was perhaps twelve or fourteen feet square. In it there was a table, four chairs, an old couch with the four legs missing and a large oil drum converted into a stove. The other room, separated by a plywood partition, was half as large and it held three single beds. The only light came through the single door and through one roughly made window behind the couch. As a consequence it was dark inside even on this cloudless summer morning. There was a crude wooden flooring with no covering of any kind.

Paul's grandmother sat on one of the chairs in a corner of the larger room. She sat unmoving and apparently unoccupied, and she gave no sign of recognition when Paul and Ken entered. Jake Onaman and Paul's mother—if he had a mother—were not in evidence.

Ken found himself trying to imagine what it would be like in that shack on a January night when the temperature dropped to thirty or forty below zero. He wondered where the cooking would be done in the winter and where the members of the family went to the bathroom. He wondered how a boy could possibly do his school homework there. He wondered what it would be like in the dampness of a rainy April day, or at dusk on Christmas Eve.

He tried to find some feature of the shack about which to express enthusiasm. He suggested that the stove would throw abundant heat and that the beds looked comfortable, and he hoped that Paul would not detect the desperation in his voice. His panic was heightened by the fact that he had already noticed that the Onaman home was the best built and most prosperous looking of all those in the village.

He felt a vast relief when Paul suggested that they depart on their trip to Duck Lake.

If the footings had been laid beforehand, it was on that day that they really began to construct the effective framework of their friendship. They paddled down the creek, portaging over the beaver dams, to Duck Lake. They swam, they fished, they explored. They made their lunch from the pickerel they caught, some raspberries picked near the water's edge and the two soft drinks. They laughed—at a cranky mother duck who sought with all her guile to lure them away from her young family, at a bullfrog that sat on a log and croaked solemnly as they paddled by, at Ken when he slipped on a moss-covered log and fell half into the water. They saw the same things. And most of all they talked.

They talked of many things, hesitantly at first and then, as reticence passed, with increasing abandon. Ken talked of the city, of school, of sports, of his friends, of his frequent loneliness in the midst of crowds. Paul talked of the men, women and children of his village, of trapping, of the harsh tricks of the weather, of the past beliefs and present doubts of his people.

He told Ken of the long winter days when he was a small boy and his old grandmother had sat with him for countless hours and taught him the stories of their people. The stories were only told in the winter because during the warm months the animals of the stories might overhear and be angry.

He told him stories of Nanabazho who made the earth and gave the Ojibways fire and taught them many things. And of Mi-shi-pi-zhiw, the Great Lynx, who lived under the water. He talked of the Ojibway belief that the Great Spirit is in all things animate and inanimate, in animals and plants and stones and water, so that all of existence is one.

He described the Mi-de-wi-win, or Great Medicine Society, and his own indoctrination into it when he had been a boy of ten. He had fasted then for a long time and cleansed himself with steam and gone off alone into the forest. And in his dreams a manitou had appeared on the fifth day. The spirit had appeared in the form of a chickadee and, on the advice of his grandmother, had been rejected. And on the ninth day, another manitou, a fox this time, had come to him and been also rejected. And then, on the tenth day, a new manitou had come and this was the otter, Ne-gig, and his grandmother had said it was a good manitou and so he had accepted it.

It was one of those rare days that seem both unbelievably short and at the same time infinitely long; one of those days that is never afterwards completely forgotten.

It occurred to Ken that Paul was as secure and confident in his ability to survive in the wilderness as he, Ken, was amid the intricacies and complexities of the city. Just as Ken knew, without conscious thought, where the traffic lights were and how much bus tickets cost, so Paul took his frame of reference from deer runs and beaver dams and the feeding habits of the pickerel.

When they parted late in the afternoon of that July day, something significant for both of them had been born. It was there in the ease of their parting and it rode with Ken as he pushed the bow of his canoe across the lake towards the cottage.

At dinner that night Ken's father had resumed the garb of the city. His white shirt, tie and black shoes looked stiff and strange in the atmosphere of the cottage. They hurried over to the station after dinner, only to find that the train was forty minutes late. Twilight was fading into night when its headlight came into sight around the long curve from the east.

Ken and his dad walked down the track past two or three cars until they found one that was less crowded. Mr. Warren shuffled forward with the others, waiting his turn to board the train. Just as he reached the step, he turned to Ken.

"I've been thinking about our talk last night," he said, "and I guess I have to admit that there is something in what you say. It's always easy to leave it to somebody else, but in this case there may not be anyone else."

73

Ken wanted to tell his father about the day he had spent with Paul and all that they had talked about, but there wasn't time. He had been going to tell him about it at dinner, but the presence of Aunt Marion had made him somehow afraid of spoiling the day.

"I just wish there was something we could do," he said.

"Maybe there is," his father said. "I'll tell you what I'll do. I'll have a talk with our company lawyer and see if he can find out what it's all about or tell us where else to go."

"Thanks, Dad," Ken said.

The conductor's call came a moment later and the train moved off into the night. Ken crossed the tracks and walked towards the lights of the store. Mr. Simpson was filling a can of coal oil outside and the store was deserted except for Moose MacGregor.

He and Ken talked for a few minutes and then, perhaps because he was so filled with the events of the day, Ken found himself telling the big forest ranger about his friendship with Paul and his sense of involvement with the Ojibways.

Moose MacGregor nodded occasionally, but, recognizing the sincerity in Ken's voice, remained silent until the boy had finished speaking.

"Yes," he said finally, "I know what you mean. They are a great people in many ways. I found that out a long time ago, and Mr. Simpson has known it since before either of us was born."

He pulled himself up and sat on the counter.

"The Indian is different, all right, and most people see the differences as weaknesses. They don't bother trying to understand them. If they did, they would find out that there's a heck of a lot to be learned from them."

"They are so much deeper than you would ever imagine," Ken said. "There's so much more to them. They're like children in some ways but, well, almost timeless, in others."

The forest ranger nodded.

"They understand a lot of things that we don't even recognize," he said. "They live closer to nature and closer to truth, and they face up to a lot of realities that we try to hide but can't eliminate."

Mr. Simpson came in and the screen door banged behind him.

"I don't know Paul very well," Moose MacGregor said, "but if he's anything like his brother, John, you've found yourself a real friend."

Chapter 9

Gradually the summer moved towards maturity. Each day, full and rich, was long, but in retrospect each week seemed to have passed quickly. The family of young ducks by the weed bed at the head of the lake moved through the water with more assurance now. The first grasshoppers appeared in the long grass near the station. The pickerel moved out into deeper water. The blueberries were ripening. The cattails stood brown and firm. The wild rice was filling. The dandelions had gone to seed.

Day after day the skies were deep blue and cloudless. Occasionally clouds formed up ominously on the horizon, but after that savage storm on the day when Ken and Paul first went fishing together, no rain fell on Kinniwabi. Each day the sun burned down, drying grass and shrubs and trees. Here and there a cedar tree took on a tinge of brown and along the margin of the lake an occasional branch turned yellow or scarlet—a premature foretaste of fall. The deer and moose moved down into the lowlands in search of green grass.

In front of the forest ranger's house and office there was a sign with an arrow to indicate the degree of forest fire danger. By the middle of the month Moose MacGregor had moved it hard over to the bright scarlet band, indicating maximum hazard.

Not a breeze was stirring as Ken walked down the path to the dock one morning towards the end of July. A cicada droned back on the ridge, but otherwise all nature seemed to be at rest. The varnished seat of the boat was so hot under the sun that he had to get a cushion from the boathouse before he could sit down.

There were no other boats on the lake as he turned the point towards the station. There was no sign of life over at the Indian village across the lake—even the almost perpetual columns of smoke from the cooking fires seemed to have been stilled. He and Paul had spent a great deal of time together since his first visit to the village, but today Paul was away on some errand with his father.

There was a light blue haze on the rocky hills behind the station and it seemed to Ken that there was a touch of smoke in the air. He had heard that there were several forest fires in the vicinity, including a big one over near Eagle Lake. With the continuing dryness and the relentless heat, it felt as if the whole world was ready to ignite. Like a vast tinder box, Ken thought.

At the store Ken learned that there had been yet another robbery.

"Judge Burnham's place," Mr. Simpson told him. "They broke in there last night and stole a boatload of stuff. Even took an old shotgun that hasn't been fired in fifty years. If they try to shoot that, they'll blow up the whole lake. I wouldn't be surprised if there was a bird's nest in the barrel."

Mr. Simpson sank back on his chair behind the counter. In spite of his years, the old storekeeper usually seemed impervious to physical strain, but the heat was having an influence even on him.

"This time they've really got people steamed up," he said. "Apparently they weren't content just to take what they wanted. They tore the whole place apart. Broke windows, smashed dishes, threw the judge's books around. Just needless destruction. And the old judge is well liked around here. Everybody feels he's had enough tough luck with his wife dying last year and him in the hospital now, himself. It's a real shame."

"It makes you wonder how long these robberies are going to go on," Ken said. "You'd think something would be done about it."

"Something is going to be done," Mr. Simpson told him. "They've called a meeting for tonight at the station. I'm not sure it's the right thing to do, though. When people get riled up and have meetings, they sometimes get carried away by each other's speeches. Then, the first thing you know, they do something silly."

When Ken walked along the station platform on his way back to the boat, the notice calling the meeting caught his eye. Printed laboriously in large, block letters, it was signed by Mr. Palmer, the secretary of the Kinniwabi Cottagers' Association. Ken stood in the shade of the station platform and read it. The meeting was scheduled for eight o'clock that evening. It had been called, the notice said, "because of the recurring instances of robbery and vandalism" and would lead, it was hoped, "to some positive action which will end these outrages."

As Ken stood there he heard voices from inside the station, voices which, though tightly controlled, reflected inner anger and bitterness.

". . . told you again and again," Mr. Morley was saying. "You know I don't like to argue with you, Janet, but I have to protect you for your own good."

78

"But protect me from what?" Janet Morley asked. "I just don't understand you. John Onaman and I have been friends since I got out of my crib. We'll never be any more than that, but I don't see why you insist that we be any less."

"Because I want you to be something," her father said. "I've worked at this job so that I could send you away from here to get an education. I want you to grow up with nice people and nice things. I wish you never had to come back to this place, but when you do come back I'm at least going to make sure that you don't waste your time with riffraff like that Indian."

"But—oh, what's the use?" Janet asked. "You've got a real mania about the Indians and nothing I say about John is going to get through to you. But, I'm sorry, Dad—he's going to be a friend of mine in my mind, whatever you say."

"Maybe so," her father said. "Maybe so—but at least I can keep him from hanging around here. And I will, if it's the last . . . "

Ken heard the rear door of the station close and a moment later saw Janet walking slowly, her head down, towards the lake. Ken, embarrassed and saddened by what he had overheard, waited until she was out of sight and then went down to the boat.

As Ken returned across the lake after dinner that evening, the sun still burned down from a cloudless sky but it had become a fiery red ball. There was now a definite pall of smoke over the hills and down to the tops of the trees. The acrid smell of it was strong in his nostrils and he could feel it in his eyes.

When he reached the station the dock was already lined with boats and the station platform was crowded with cottagers. Two subjects were on everyone's lips—the smoke and the series of robberies.

The scene seemed strangely unreal to Ken. The unnatural sun, the ominous, oppressive blanket of the smoke and, most of all, the crowd of people, shifting uncomfortably as they waited for the meeting to begin, had transformed Kinniwabi into something alien.

The eastbound transcontinental train roared through the station just before eight o'clock, its windows giving blurred and fleeting images of its passengers as it sped by. Shortly afterwards Mr. Palmer called the meeting to order. Standing on a baggage wagon at one end of the platform and appearing slightly self-conscious, he asked for attention. Conversations dwindled and the people moved slowly to form an uneven semicircle around him.

"You all know the purpose of this meeting," he said. "These robberies have been going on all summer and it seemed to some of us that it was time we did something about it."

"Somebody has to do something about it," a voice from the edge of the crowd said. "That mess they made of Judge Burnham's place was the last straw."

There were faint murmurs of assent from all sides.

"There's no reason why this should be a formal meeting," Mr. Palmer said. "In fact if it was a formal meeting, I wouldn't know how to run it anyway."

Light laughter ran through the crowd, but there was still an uneasy feeling. They were not used to acting as a group. There was a prolonged discussion which, though varying in its degree of perception and articulateness, added little to the two conclusions established by the chairman's introductory remarks—the series of robberies was unfortunate and something would have to be done about them.

"Isn't this really a matter for the authorities?" a woman asked finally. She seemed embarrassed at having spoken up. "I mean, really, that's what the police are for. Shouldn't we call them in?"

"The police ought to be able to look after it pretty quick," Wilbur Crowe said. "After all, it's plain enough who did it, isn't it?"

All eyes turned towards the speaker, who stood with one foot on a station bench, leaning back against the wall.

"How do you mean?" someone asked.

"Well, now, I know you people might not like to come right out and say it, being reasonable and all, but any of us could tell the policemen where to look now, couldn't we?"

"I agree with you, Wilbur," D. R. Morley said. "After all, there's no mystery about it—no mystery at all."

"Not to me, Mr. Morley," the big man said. He moved his head slightly to one side towards the Indian encampment. "Plain as the nose on your face as far as I'm concerned."

"Certainly it is," said the station agent. "Obviously it isn't any of us, and nobody can get in here from outside without my knowing about it. It has to be them."

"Has to be who?" someone else asked.

There was a pause, and then Wilbur Crowe spoke up again. "Well, I don't mind comin' right out and saying it," he said. "It's them Indians and breeds down the shore. Everybody knows what they are, don't they?"

"Wait a minute, here," Mr. Simpson said, his eyes narrow and a sharp edge to his voice. "You haven't any right to make an accusation like that, Crowe. I protest against everything you've said and insinuated."

"I just thought you might, Mr. Simpson," Wilbur Crowe said. "After all, you're a friend of theirs, aren't you? Birds of a feather, I always say."

There was a murmur of resentment, for the old storekeeper was much liked and highly respected.

"No reason to be insulting, Wilbur," Mr. Morley said. "We all want to hear Mr. Simpson's opinion. But it's true—who else could it be but the Indians?"

There was a long silence and then Moose MacGregor spoke up from the edge of the crowd. He had just returned from the bush. His face was unshaven, his clothes stained with ashes and soot. Smoke had darkened his complexion so that the wrinkles in his forehead stood out as white lines. There were circles of fatigue beneath his eyes and it was clear that he had slept little for many days.

"I've heard about enough of this," he said, his voice low but strong. "I didn't think a group of decent people would stand around and listen to this kind of talk."

He pushed his way gently through the crowd until he stood face to face with Wilbur Crowe.

"I'm tired, Crowe," he said evenly, "but I'm not too tired to straighten this thing out. Some of those Indians are *my* friends, all right, and I, for one, won't listen to your prejudices."

Wilbur Crowe took his foot down from the bench and straightened up. It seemed possible for a long moment that the two big men might fight there on the station platform.

"If you have any specific accusations to make, make them now," the forest ranger said. "If you have any evidence, let's hear it. And, if you haven't, you better be quiet."

"I'll speak up when the time comes," Wilbur Crowe said. "I'll have plenty to say when the police get here."

"That'll be a change, anyway," Mr. Simpson said. "Usually all you want to say to the police is good-bye."

"Wait, now. Wait, wait, wait," Mr. Palmer said, trying to restore some measure of order. "There isn't any sense to our fighting among ourselves. The only thing to do is to call in the police and let them handle it. Then anyone who has anything to say can tell it to them."

It was agreed that a telegram should be sent right away asking for police assistance.

Moose MacGregor stood looking steadily into Wilbur Crowe's eyes for another long minute. Les Crowe and Dinnie Hackett, the latter hesitantly, had moved to Wilbur Crowe's side. Finally the big forest ranger turned away.

"I've got too much on my mind to deal with you now," he said, "but if there's any more of this kind of thing, you'll be hearing from me later."

He moved wearily through the crowd which was slowly beginning to disperse. Then he stopped and looked towards the east, his eyes troubled.

"If an east wind gets up overnight," he said to no one in particular, "we'll all have something more to worry about than these robberies. That fire's burning like somebody poured gasoline on it."

Chapter 10

The next morning, the sun rose as it had set—a mammoth red ball in a cloudless sky. The smoke had increased greatly through the night. The heavy acridity of it had made sleep fitful for many people in the cottages around Lake Kinniwabi. Children had pitched and tossed, and old people had coughed and struggled for breath.

At first, in the stillness of the early morning, the dominant sun was reflected perfectly in the dead calm of the water. Then a breeze stirred the topmost leaves of a poplar tree on a ridge behind the Indian encampment. It was only the merest movement of air, but it was repeated a moment later, this time making the poplar leaves shiver more perceptibly. The branches of the pine trees swayed, gently at first and then with a wider sweep as the breeze grew. A faint ripple distorted slightly the reflection of the sun. Then a little wave danced across the water, and another, and another. Before the first breakfast fire was kindled at Kinniwabi, tiny whitecaps were breaking on the rocky point of the island in front of the Warren's cottage.

The wind, rising steadily as the morning developed, was straight out of the east.

Ken awakened to the sound of a pine bow brushing angrily against the roof over his head. Then, going to the window, he saw the waves beginning to roll up the lake. The smoke was gone now, but there was still a distinct smell in the air.

At breakfast the talk was of the fire burning at Eagle Lake and of Moose MacGregor's solemn warning of the previous evening. Even the dramatic meeting was forgotten.

Just as they were finishing their meal, a motorboat came around the point. It slowed as it approached their dock and they heard a voice shouting.

"I wonder what they want," Ken said, rising from the table and starting down the path. As he neared the dock, he saw that there were two men in the boat—Moose MacGregor and John Onaman.

"Hurry over to the station," MacGregor called. John Onaman, in the stern, didn't shut the motor off completely, but let it idle with the gearshift in neutral. "The fire's moving this way fast. There's a special train leaving to fight it in a half hour or so. We need every pair of hands we can get. Wear some old clothes and hurry right over."

He signaled to John Onaman, who immediately threw the motor into gear and turned the throttle to high. The bow of the boat rose abruptly as they roared away towards the next cottage. The fire ranger had not even waited for a reply.

Ken hurried up to the cottage.

"I have to go right away," he said. "The fire is worse and moving this way. There's a special train in a half an hour, and I've got to go. Everybody has to go."

Aunt Marion protested against his going, but his mother, not without some anxiety in her eyes, agreed that there was no alternative. It had been clear from Moose MacGregor's voice that the situation was desperate.

He put on an old pair of slacks, a shirt he had worn for painting and a battered fedora that his father wore fishing. Several other boats were converging on the station as he headed into the gradually building waves. The scene there was one of uncertain activity. The work train, dispatched from the city, had already arrived and stood on the siding. There was a baggage car, a couple of old wooden passenger coaches, a cook car and a caboose. At the door of the baggage car several men were checking over equipment—picks, shovels, axes, burlap bags, chains and other articles. Others were milling around, wanting to help but disorganized and vague as to what was expected of them. Moose MacGregor was talking to the engineer and Mr. Morley.

"We'll just have to do the best we can and see what develops," Ken heard him say. "If we can't check it, the fire could be here by nightfall with this wind."

"The railway has given us authority to use the train for evacuating the women and children if we have to," the station agent said.

"Okay," MacGregor said. "We'll move the train back this way as it becomes necessary. If it does look like we'll have to get everybody out of here, I'll send someone back with a message in time for you to warn them."

"They're going to keep the main line open for you," said the station agent, "even if they have to hold up the transcontinentals."

"If the fire swings south and cuts the track, they may be held up for quite a while," the forest ranger said wryly. "Right now it's only a mile or so to the north."

As they talked a group of Indians came walking down the track from their village. There were a couple of dozen of them, ranging in age from older boys to men whose shoulders were stooped under their years. Ken saw Paul in the forefront of the group, walking with his father.

"Good," said Moose MacGregor. "They'll be a big help

back there. We can use some professionals. Okay, I think everybody is here that's coming. Let's get on board and be on our way."

Ken and Paul met as they stood waiting to board the train. There was little conversation, the ominous proximity of the fire hanging over them like the smoke which had so recently been dispelled by the wind.

The railway coaches were old and the hard wooden seats would have been uncomfortable had there been time to consider this factor. The train moved away from the station with a jerk like a freight train and gradually picked up speed.

Ken and Paul sat side by side, watching ahead for signs of the fire. They had not long to wait. The edge of it was only some six miles away from Kinniwabi and the dense smoke was soon visible just north of the railway line. A few minutes later the train slowed to a stop. As he jumped down beside the track, the heat from the fire hit Ken like a blast from a suddenly opened oven. It was a searing, scorching heat that tore at his throat and took away his breath. The malevolent power of it was staggering.

Moose MacGregor assembled them there beside the train and divided them into groups, each with an experienced woodsman in charge. Ken and Paul found themselves in the same group, with John Onaman as their leader. A minute later they headed into the bush, walking in single file along a deer trail which skirted a meadow and curved away in the direction of the fire.

As they walked, the heat built up to almost unbearable intensity. All conversation had now completely died away. It was hard enough merely to breathe. After a few minutes they heard the fire for the first time. It came to them as a roar, growing gradually in intensity and punctuated by staccato reports as sharp as a high-powered rifle. The noise was unbelievable.

After a while they came to the bank of a narrow stream. In normal times it would have been a pleasant, pastoral break in the forest, its water bubbling gently over moss-covered rocks. Now the continuing drought had reduced the flow of water to a dispirited trickle.

"Okay," Moose MacGregor called to them. "This is the plan. It's not much, but it's all we can do. This stream is a narrow barrier between us and the fire. As it is, it's not nearly wide enough to do any good. We're going to try to widen it before the fire reaches here."

He paused for a moment, studying his oddly assorted crew of fire fighters.

"We haven't got much time," he said, "but if we work hard, we might just get the break wide enough to slow up the fire. It's going to be hard work, but do the best you can."

They strung themselves out along the bank of the little stream. The equipment in the baggage car of the train had included four portable chain saws which ran on gasoline motors similar to the outboards on their boats back at the lake. Moose MacGregor, John Onaman and two other forest rangers who had come over from Bishop Falls handled the saws. The rest pitched in to haul tree trunks and branches back into the forest as fast as trees were felled. Some worked with axes, cutting down bushes and small trees.

It was desperately hard work. Branches tore at them as they moved back and forward in the dense underbrush. Mosquitoes, seemingly impervious to the smoke, buzzed around them. Deadfalls tripped them up and crevices in the rock wrenched their ankles. Berry bushes caught at their clothes and hidden roots caught at their feet.

The surefooted competence of the Indians stood them in good stead. Paul and his father, working nearby, seemed to Ken as unaffected by the heat and thick bush as they had been when the three of them had been carrying logs to re-build the Warrens' dock. While heat and fatigue dragged at the throats and legs and chests of Ken and the other cot-tagers, the Indians kept working as though impervious to hardship. John Onaman went from tree to tree, on and on, without pause.

Progress was heartbreakingly slow. After a while, Ken lost track of time. It seemed to him that he had been work-ing silently there in the bush for days or even weeks. And, for a long time, the break they were trying to make on the banks of the unnamed little stream remained frustratingly without form or dimension. But gradually the western bank of the stream was cleared away. The heat of the fire grew steadily more intense as the flames moved towards them. At last Moose MacGregor told them it was time to move out. He had to shout to make himself heard. The cut by then was a miraculously clear swath, perhaps thirty feet wide, through the forest. So long in taking shape, it now neverthe-less gave them reason for confidence as they picked up their tools and dragged themselves to a rock ridge a quarter of a mile to the west. There they sat silently in the shade and watched apprehensively as the fire moved inexhorably to-wards their fire break.

"I hope it works," Paul said.

"Me, too," said Ken. "I haven't got the strength to move again if it doesn't."

The roar of the fire was loud 'in their ears now. They could see the flames leaping from treetop to treetop. The fierceness of it was demoniacal, and its power seemed too great for any force or any tactic to deny.

Yet, for a time it seemed that their firebreak was going to work. The flames came to the edge of the stream, roared angrily there and stopped. The trees along its edge were consumed in the terrible heat, faded away to fiery ashes and collapsed. On the near edge of their break the forest still stood, green and safe. They had checked the fire. Some of the weariness gave way to a faint pride.

And then, in one terrible instant, the fire made a mockery of all their efforts. One moment the holocaust was at bay. The next, the dry top of a cedar on their side of the break suddenly exploded into flame. The incredible heat had traveled underground along one root, transferred to another, and then up through the resin in the cedar tree until it touched the browning branches at the very top. There, like tinder, the dry leaves suddenly ignited. In an instant the fire had crossed the break and was again a living, consuming monster—this time on their side of the little stream.

"Okay," said Moose MacGregor, his voice touched with weariness and despair, "let's try again. Everybody fall back."

They made their next stand beside a deep gully, formed countless ages ago when the last ice age had moved over Kinniwabi. Again the frantic, seemingly disorganized activity finally and surprisingly resulted in a treeless moat in front of the advancing fire. Again the flames hesitated on the far side of the desperate ditch. Again hopes were stirred. Maybe they had won. And then again, as hope began to stir in weary hearts, the fire leaped across their wall of space.

Twice more that afternoon they moved back, summoning their strength and their determination. Twice more they sweated and cursed and stumbled and sighed. Twice more they retreated to watch the fire come up against their breastworks. And twice more the irresistible flames leaped contemptuously over their sweat and their toil and their determination and hurried on towards Kinniwabi.

Their hands were now raw things, torn and blistered and bruised. Their throats were dry and sore. Their faces were dirty and streaked with perspiration and ashes and pine pitch. Their backs ached and their hearts pounded. They moved, not as human beings but as automatons, doing what they had to do, not because they had hope but because there was no other course. The fire was, of course, irresistible and it was absurd and preposterous to lay their feeble protestations before it. The fire would conquer all and consume the world and there was nothing they could do about it. But equally, they could not avoid going on with their efforts. Side by side, Ken and Paul, Moose MacGregor and John Onaman, Wilbur Crowe and George White Bear, old and young, devout and profane, they worked on silently, hopelessly, on the verge of complete exhaustion.

In the late afternoon, far over the horizon behind the fire and quite unknown to them, a tiny cloud formed and moved slowly across the otherwise vacant sky. It was a mere wisp of condensation, almost transparent against the blue. An airline pilot, winging eastward, would not have considered it a threat to the game scheduled for that evening. A farmer, despairing of his parched fields, would have found little ground for hope in it.

Yet, behind the cloud, beneath the horizon, there were other tiny puffs of white. As the shadows stretched out from

91

the shoreline across Lake Kinniwabi, the clouds joined forces, growing gradually into a bank and darkening in color. As the wind died away in early evening the formation reached slowly across the eastern horizon.

Deep in the forest, the embattled and weary fire fighters were unaware of the clouds building in the sky until they reached out and touched the setting sun. Then Moose Mac-Gregor let his saw rest for a moment and looked skyward. He saw the clouds moving across an opening between the trees, their edges beginning to roll as thunderheads formed.

"It can't be," he said quietly. "It just can't be."

The others stopped their work and stood silently or slumped wearily to the ground, all eyes turned upwards. Their own efforts had proven so fruitless and their own strength was so completely dissipated, that by common consent they transformed any hope they had left to the darkening mass in the late afternoon sky. The break they were cutting, had they been able to finish it before the fire reached them, would have been their last try. After that there would have been no choice but to evacuate, picking up the women and children on the way and admitting complete surrender to the fire. Now, salvation, not of their making, might be at hand.

The clouds rolled slowly across the sky. It grew steadily darker. The uppermost tongues of flame were now clearly visible as the fire pressed towards them again. The clouds built and took on depth. Jagged lightning streaked down to the horizon. Thunder rolled majestically across the sky. At other times they would have hurried from the forest because of the danger of lightning and falling trees. Now they were too weary to do more than sit silently and watch.

For long anxious moments it seemed that the storm was going to pass over with threats and bravado but no rain.

"Please," MacGregor said, half to himself.

And then the first drops pattered lightly on the leaves above them. Every head tilted more sharply upwards and then dropped again as the rain faltered. Then a sharp crack of thunder echoed through the forest and suddenly the sky seemed to open. A solid curtain of rain blanketed them— harsh, driving, cold, wonderful rain. It ran over their heads and down their faces. It plastered their dirty clothes to their bodies. It saturated the world around them.

"Thank God," a voice said quietly.

The rain poured down. It made little rivulets between the rocks. It dripped from leaves. It soaked into the parched earth and then made little pools in the low places where the moss grew.

For a long time the fire fighters stayed there, too drained, physically and emotionally, to move. And then, finally, they began to walk slowly along the trail through the gathering darkness toward the work train.

They walked silently, singly and in pairs. Ken walked with Paul. Old Mr. Simpson walked, shoulders slumping, beside the hulking form of Wilbur Crowe. Les Crowe and Jacob Onaman went out side by side.

And every now and then each of them looked up at the sky and let the blessed rain run down his face.

Chapter 11

The shared adventure of the forest fire was one more bond in the developing friendship between Ken and Paul. As July slipped past and gave way to August, they spent more and more time together. They swam, fished, picked berries, shared each other's chores. Much of the time they spent in exploring the area around Kinniwabi, ranging sometimes far into the uncharted forest north of the lake. Several times they camped overnight. They took their canoes, sometimes Ken's and sometimes Paul's along rivers and across lakes that few besides the Ojibway had seen. The trout stream running into Cygnet Lake was their favorite discovery.

The lake was a tough four-hour journey from Kinniwabi, involving several long portages and an exhausting paddle up the Beaver River on the way back. They had been in to Cygnet Lake twice before they found the stream. Its mouth was choked with driftwood and almost grown over with willows, and it was only by sheer luck that they stumbled on it. They had been looking for small green frogs to use as bait for bass.

The stream made up in beauty upstream for its unimpressive appearance where it joined the lake. Dropping sharply down from a rock ridge to the north, it consisted of a series of terraced pools, deep, dark pockets of water connected by bubbling little waterfalls. High pines arched over the stream and it was always cool there, even on the hottest days. The pools were full of ravenous little brook trout, none of them over ten inches in length, but fat, full of fighting spirit, and firm and tasty in a frying pan.

Paul spent a good deal of time at the Warren cottage, where he was liked and respected by Ken's mother and tolerated, with sometimes poorly concealed disapproval, by his Aunt Marion. At the Ojibway village, Ken gradually won a degree of acceptance, although it was some time before he began to realize it. Through his first several visits none of the other Indians spoke to him or gave any sign that they were aware of his presence. Ken came to recognize several faces there and knew several people by name, but other eyes avoided his whenever he sought to exchange greetings and his smile of recognition usually went unreturned and apparently unseen. This reticence—he had originally interpreted it as hostility—gradually began to break down, and he penetrated it first through the children. The first chink in the wall came one morning when Ken and Paul became involved in a baseball game the children were playing at the back of the clearing. From then on the children called him by name and it was not long before some of the adults followed their example.

They talked a great deal that summer—sometimes sitting in the bottom of the canoe as it drifted gently, sometimes lying on a flat rock in the hot sun, sometimes watching the moon across the lake long after the last light had blinked out in the cottages.

Ken told Paul about the city. He talked of the things that fascinated him and that he found good. He described the university and the learning there, he spoke of sports, of movies he had seen, of television programs and of his friends. And he brought up things that he found ugly, unfair and frightening. They talked of the atomic bomb as one of the by-products of science and knowledge, and wondered, half jokingly, if they would ever have to go to war together because of it. Paul asked many questions about these things and sometimes they argued at length over them.

Paul, in his turn, told Ken much about his people. He spoke of their past, spoke of it with pride. Of the greatness they had known. Of their beliefs. Of the strength and beauty in their legends. He spoke, with some humor but also with some respect, of the omens many of his people still accepted. It was never good, he said, to return to the lodge for something that you had forgotten because that would bring bad luck. No woman must be allowed to touch the things that were used for hunting and fishing if one wanted to return to the village with food. It was bad luck to see a place where a mole had burrowed for that meant that a close friend or relative might die. And, if your leg jerked in your sleep, that was bad, too, because it signified that you would soon have to run for your life.

And he spoke with fear and sometimes with resentment of the plight of his people and of what the future might hold for them. They talked of this many times, saying the same things that many other people had said, and, like them, coming to no hopeful conclusions.

They talked as much as they did, not in·spite of the fact that they were different, but because of it, and because, in spite of all the disparities in their mutual experience, they were alike in their ages and in their wonder at the sun and moon and wind and heat and rain and all the things of nature that went to make up that summer and their common universe.

Paul's fifteenth birthday fell during the first few days of

August. He did not mention this in anticipation of a party but rather as a fact that would mean he and Ken would be the same age once again. When Ken learned of it, he determined to buy Paul a birthday present, the first, he suspected, that his friend would ever receive. He gave his father some money that he had saved during the previous winter and asked him to buy a wristwatch while he was in the city. Then, on Paul's birthday, he paddled over to the Ojibway village. For the first time in many days he was embarrassed and not sure what to do. In the end he simply handed the blue paper package to his friend. Paul opened it, putting the paper in his pocket. He took out the box, turned back the lid, took out the watch and put it on his right wrist. Then he wound it and turned the hands to approximately the correct time. He said nothing. At no time then or in the future was the watch mentioned. At no time in the future did Ken ever see Paul without it.

Ken gradually learned some words of Ojibway. He did not develop any understanding of the structure or grammar of the language, but after a while he was able to identify some common objects. He came to know that *me-kee-nouck* meant turtle, *ah-ne-moosh* meant dog, *mah-quh* was bear, and *wash-ke-zhe* signified deer. With Paul he always referred to his canoe as *gee-mon*, and when it rained he would point to the sky and say *"gim-e-waun."*

Early in August two policemen càme to Kinniwabi on the evening train. They came in response to the request sent as a result of the cottagers' meeting and they stayed over until the following day. Ken learned from Mr. Simpson that they talked to many people, including as many victims as were at Kinniwabi. There were the usual rumors that arrests had been made, or were imminent, but in the long run the situation was unchanged on their departure. Wilbur Crowe suggested, after they had gone, that the authorities had no interest in such a remote place as Kinniwabi and that they would never have come at all except for the fact that some of the cottagers had influence in the city. Mr. Morley more or less endorsed this view and expressed his belief that, if anything were to be done about the robberies, they would have to do it themselves.

There were no further thefts and, while not completely forgotten, the series of robberies lost some interest as a topic of conversation around the station.

For Ken the summer was speeding by far too quickly. It was hard for him to accept the fact that his father's vacation had already come and gone. He realized one day, with a shock, that two-thirds of the summer was already gone and that in just over three weeks' time they would be returning to the city.

The adults' thoughts were turning that way. Newspaper advertisements for August sales and autumn wardrobes began to hold increasing fascination for Aunt Marion. She remembered a late August dental appointment. His mother started to fuss about getting the house in order for fall. When she proposed that they should all go to the city for a few days, Ken decided he didn't want to leave Kinniwabi until he absolutely had to. He begged to be allowed to stay on at the cottage alone. The boats and maintenance were his responsibility already and he could manage meals with the help of a well-stocked refrigerator. "All right," his father said when appealed to. "You're old enough now. Just keep busy and stay out of mischief."

That wasn't difficult for Ken. The days were so full that he could scarcely comprehend their passing. There never seemed to be enough time to accomplish all that he wanted to do.

One thing that he did achieve was a basic familiarity with his new camera and developing kit. He took several rolls of film, some colored and some black and white. Developing his exposures was a problem at the lake because the Warren cottage had no electricity, but his friendship with Moose MacGregor stood him in good stead. The forest ranger's cabin tapped power from the line that followed the railway and Ken was able to develop two or three rolls of film there with some success. The rest he sent into the city with his father. By experimentation he learned what his camera would do and by the middle of August he had taken some quite creditable pictures. He particularly liked working with the flashbulb attachment. It intrigued him to be able to take pictures in the dark and he liked the dramatic effects made possible by this phenomenon.

Each week, from Sunday night to Friday evening, Ken waited hopefully and impatiently to hear the news of Empirico's plans from his father. For a long time nothing happened. The word each weekend was that the company lawyer was looking into the matter as far as his other duties and his contacts would permit.

"I wish I could tell you something more definite," his father would say, "but you have to remember that the lawyer has a lot of other duties—duties he's paid for. This business with the Ojibway is just something that he is doing as a favor to me. I can't push him too much."

Ken understood this. He was grateful for the fact that *something* was being done. But, like many another person before him, he found himself growing impatient at the law's delay.

"The real problem," his father told him one weekend, "is that nobody knows where to go for specific information. Our lawyer is a pretty honest guy and he's smart. I think he's really trying to help us, but where do you go for information that nobody seems to care about? This thing may be important to you, and maybe to me, but who else cares about it? Nobody, as far as I can find out—except Empirico, of course. And I'm not even sure *they* are interested, except in so far as the law says that the land belongs to them."

"I know," Ken said. "It's good of the lawyer to take an interest. After all, he's never even seen Kinniwabi and he wouldn't know Paul from Adam. But it is discouraging. You'd think that finding out the facts would be simple enough."

"I guess the law is never simple," his father said.

The days and weeks sped by and suddenly the first genuine flash of color appeared in a maple tree on the far point of the island. Summer was clearly on the wane, even though the sun still burned down through the days, and the path of the August moon was still soft and languid across the gentle surface of the lake.

One Friday night, as Ken rounded the point on the way to the station to pick up Mr. Warren from the weekend train, he noticed that the sun had already dipped behind the western trees. A few weeks earlier he had been able to take his father over to the cottage and share a late dinner with him before darkness descended. Now the shadows were already long before he reached the station dock and the headlight of the diesel engine cut a path through the gathering dusk as it slowed for Kinniwabi. The lights in the day coaches and diner were on, bright rectangles in the settling twilight.

The shadows of the shoreline were already indistinct in the gathering dusk as they reached the cottage that evening and Ken had to use the flashlight to find the dock. They ate their dinner in the flickering light of the coal oil lamps. Afterwards his father lit a cigarette as he sipped at his coffee.

"Well, Ken," he said, "I've finally got something definite from the company lawyer. But I'm afraid it's not good news. It seems there is a deed dating back to about the beginning of this century. Empirico bought out the rights granted by this deed. The Indians, as far as I can learn, had no part in the deal. But there is no doubt that Empirico has title. The only question concerns the description of their holdings."

He took a sip of coffee before he continued.

"Apparently the problem centers around the location of a certain creek referred to as the western boundary of the company's holdings," he said. "The deed says that the company owns the land eastward from this creek clear to the railway property at the station. The only creek there is on the north side of Lake Kinniwabi is that little stream they call Northey's Creek. That is clearly on the west side of the Indian village and therefore the land they are living on belongs to Empirico. It's as simple as that."

Ken sat in silence, toying with his apple pie but with little taste for it.

"I wish it had turned out otherwise," his father said, "but we might just as well face it. There is no other creek on that side of Kinniwabi. There isn't even a trickle of water anywhere else."

Ken said nothing. Despair gripped his heart. His mind ran along the north shore of the lake, from the Indian encampment eastward. There was nothing else resembling a creek. No amount of wishful thinking could change that.

"We've done our best," his father said, "and I'm glad we gave it a try. But there's no sense kidding ourselves—the Indians don't have a case at all. Empirico is right and there is nothing we can do to make it different."

Chapter 12

It was a relief to Ken when Paul came by the next morning to say that he would be working for a few days with his father on a job down the lake. It meant a short reprieve in communicating the grim news. The two boys arranged to go fishing together on Wednesday afternoon.

That morning Ken woke early, but he didn't get out of bed for a long time. The sun, filtering through the pine boughs outside his window, told him that it would be a good morning for a swim, but he couldn't work up any enthusiasm for the idea. He considered the possibility of going fishing. Perhaps the quiet solitude of morning on the lake would be good for him. But somehow fishing didn't seem worth the trouble either. He put his hands behind his head and watched the flickering patterns of light on the ceiling. A fly buzzed angrily through the rafters. Where did he find the strength to be so energetic?

His father's news of the previous weekend had come as a real blow, and with it something seemed to have gone out of the summer. It had been foolish, Ken told himself, to suppose that they might be able to do something about the plight of the Ojibway. Powerful forces were at work—confident, professional, knowledgeable forces—and the result had been inevitable. It was good of his father and the company lawyer to have tried, but it had probably all been pretty useless. Still, maybe it was better to have tried and failed than to have done nothing at all.

Well, one thing was certain—there was nothing to be gained by moping around in bed. He swung his feet out onto the floor. As he dressed, he looked around the room, remembering other mornings of that summer. His eyes fell on the open windows overlooking the lake and he recalled the whispering voices he had heard in the still darkness of the early morning hours that night three weeks earlier. Again, for a fleeting instant, identification trembled at the threshold of his awareness. And again it danced tantalizingly away.

He forced himself to eat some breakfast in the kitchen and then went down to the boathouse. Paul was coming over later in the day and he wondered how he would break the news to him. He had told his friend that the lawyer was looking into the matter. Perhaps, he thought, I was wrong to raise his hopes. But his own enthusiasm had been kindled and it had been impossible to resist passing along some of it to Paul. Well, there was nothing to do but come right out with it. No amount of beating around the bush would change the fact that the faint spark had been snuffed out.

He had promised his father to spend the morning catching up with some chores. For once it would be good to have some work to do. He threw himself into it with such zeal that his disappointment was temporarily forgotten.

After lunch he went down to the dock to wait for Paul. He sat on the deck of the motorboat for a while, glancing occasionally across the lake for a sign of Paul's red canoe.

An hour passed and a strong feeling that something was wrong superimposed itself on his generally low spirits. After a while he put away the book he was reading, got into his canoe and headed across the lake towards the Ojibway village. A few minutes later he pulled his canoe up on the now familiar muddy beach and started up the path. He passed two or three people whom he had come to know, but they did not mirror his smile or return his words of greeting. In each case they looked away from him as if he were not there.

At the Onaman's house Paul's father was standing on a box, making some repairs to the roof.

"Hello, Mr. Onaman," Ken called out. "Is Paul around?"

The little man went on with his work, giving no acknowledgment of Ken's presence. He was wearing the same cap and the same shirt as he had when Ken had first seen him at the beginning of the summer.

"Hello," Ken repeated. "Is Paul around?"

For another long moment, Mr. Onaman ignored Ken. Then he turned half around, made a vague negative sound and shook his head. There was no recognition in his eyes. He returned to his work and a flash of unreasonable anger darted across the clouds of Ken's frustration and despair. That's it, he thought. Go on. Fix the roof on your rickety little house and then it will be sound and firm when they tear it down and pull you out from under it.

Ken saw some children playing farther back in the clearing and he walked towards them. By now they all knew him by name and usually ran to him. But today they seemed not to see him and darted away towards the lake. They were as light as usual in their running, but they did not laugh or shout and there seemed a sadness in their unaccustomed silence.

Puzzled and dejected, Ken wandered farther through the village. Wherever he turned, he met the same chill rejection. Here a door closed as he passed; there a group of men turned away as he approached. And there was, in addition to the silent hostility, another element in the atmosphere which hung over the village. Ken struggled to identify it. Apathy, that was it. It was as if the village had suddenly aged and, with the aging, had dried up.

He did not find Paul and at last returned to his canoe and started back across the lake. Then, on the near side of the island, pulled well up on the shore and almost hidden by bushes, he saw his friend's red canoe. Ken turned in that direction and a few moments later stepped out onto the island.

He began to work his way slowly around the shore. The ground was uneven and progress through the tangled bushes and chaotic patterns of fallen trees was slow and laborious. Overhead the jackpines closed out the sky and the shadows were deep.

Finally he came out on a small, flat point and there, sitting with his back against a rock and looking out across the lake, was Paul. Ken knew that his friend must have heard his approach, yet he gave no sign that he was aware of his presence. He went over and dropped down beside him.

"Hi," he said. "I've been looking for you."

Paul continued to look out over the water. He did not answer.

"I thought you were going to come over to my place," Ken said. "I waited a long time and then I went to find you. Why are you sitting out here?"

Paul dropped his eyes to the ground, but did not look at Ken. A train whistled far down the line towards Eagle Lake.

"Paul, for pete's sake tell me what's the matter," Ken implored. "There's something wrong. I knew it at the village, and now I'm sure. What have I done? Why are you mad at me?"

Paul reached over and broke the dried stub of a branch from a fallen cedar. He threw it into the water where it entered point first like a spear and then bobbed sharply back to the surface.

Ken waited as the silence grew between them. An overwhelming sadness and a sense of defeat urged him to withdraw. But his perplexity and a weak feeling of resentful anger held him for another long moment. Then, finally, he began to draw himself to his feet. He had half turned away when his friend spoke.

"This is where I came for my fast," he said in a low voice, "when I joined the Mid-e-wi-win and took the otter for my totem. This is where I had the dreams—here on this point."

Ken stood behind Paul, looking down at him but not knowing what to say. There was silence again for several moments.

"I will tell you," Paul said. "You have been my friend and it isn't right not to tell you. But my heart is heavy."

Ken sat down again on the rock and waited.

"Last night there was another robbery," Paul said. "Someone got into the Roxborough's place over on the point. They had gone to town for a few days and somebody forced the window and got in. They took a good deer rifle and a camp stove and some other things."

His voice was flat and emotionless.

"The police came this morning on the train," he continued. "The station agent sent a wire as soon as they found out about the theft, and two policemen came down from the city."

107

"They didn't waste any time," Ken said. "They must have been waiting for another robbery."

Paul looked at him for the first time, his eyes dark and penetrating, before he continued.

"They were only at the station for a few minutes," he said, "and then they came straight to the village. It was as if they knew what they were going to do before they got here."

"What happened?" Ken asked. "What did they want at the village?"

"They came," Paul said in a low voice, "to arrest my brother. They came to get John and his friend, Henry Two Turtles. They came to take them away."

"Oh, no," Ken said. "Not John. Why him? What proof did they have?"

Paul snorted lightly and looked at Ken. There was a bitter smile on his lips that Ken had never seen before.

"Why do they need proof?" he asked. "What has that got to do with it? John is an Indian, isn't he? Isn't that proof enough?"

Dismayed, Ken looked at his friend and then found that, in spite of himself, he had to turn his eyes away. The awareness of the other news he had to tell, news that for now could not be told, was heavy on his heart. Perhaps Paul was right. But, no, he thought, it can't really be that bad. They must at least think they have some evidence.

"No, Paul," he said slowly, "I don't believe that that's the only reason."

Paul tilted his head back slightly and a faint, bitter laugh came from his throat.

"You see?" he said. "You think there must be something to it, too. It's an Indian, so you are ready to believe it."

Ken shook his head vehemently.

"No, no, no," he said. "That's not what I mean at all. I'm not ready to believe it and I don't believe it. What I meant was that the police must *think* they have something to go on—some evidence that John and Henry did it. They're wrong, but there must be a reason. They can't just arrest anybody because they feel like it."

He kicked at some moss with his heel.

"After all the police know that they'll have to prove it in court," he said.

"They'll prove it," Paul said angrily. "They'll find a way to pin it on them. I know. I've seen it happen before."

Ken found himself wondering if his friend had ever cried.

"Now listen to me, Paul," he said slowly, choosing his words with great care. "Paul, you've got to listen. Do you hear me?"

His friend turned at last and looked at him.

"You've got to get this through your head," Ken said. "I believe in John and I want to help him. Lots of people in those cottages over there would help, too, if they could. They don't all believe the things you say."

Paul was listening, but Ken did not know whether or not his words were really penetrating his friend's despair.

"You're making the same mistakes you say the police are making," he said. "You're jumping to conclusions before you know the whole story. It's not going to do any good to sit here and brood about it. Let's go over to the station and find out what is really going on."

"I don't want to go over," Paul said. "Everybody will look at me and whisper things behind my back. It's better just to forget it."

109

"Well, you can forget it if you want to," Ken said, pulling himself to his feet. "You can sit here and mope and think everybody is against you, but I'm not going to sit with you."

He started back towards his canoe.

"I'm going to go over and see what I can find out," he said over his shoulder.

He moved to the edge of the trees at the back of the rocky point and then stopped and turned around.

"Are you coming with me?" he called back.

For a long moment he waited, watching Paul. His friend sat, unmoving, looking out again across the water. Then Ken turned and began to pick his way through the underbrush. He felt terribly weary and it was hard work fighting his way toward the canoe. It reminded him of the first few days he had known Paul, when the two of them and Mr. Onaman had hauled the logs out of the bush for the new dock. How long ago that seemed now.

He came out at last in the little bay where the two canoes were drawn up. He had pushed his canoe back into the water and was pulling it around parallel to the shore so that he could step into it, when he heard a sound back in the bush. He straightened up then, holding the canoe by its bow rope and listening. He heard other sounds and then, a moment later, he saw Paul's checked shirt coming towards him. His friend's head was down as he picked his way through the tangled undergrowth and over the rocks. Finally he stood beside Ken and raised his head, so that their eyes met.

"I'll come," he said. "I don't want to and it won't do any good, but I'll come."

Ken nodded. He wanted to reach out and put his hand on his friend's shoulder. He wanted to say that the whole thing

110

would work out all right. But he knew that it might not work out that way at all. He knew that Paul was quite probably right.

"Okay," he said. "Let's go then."

They pushed off in their canoes, one red and one green, and paddled side by side in silence across the lake towards the far shore.

Chapter 13

The station, usually deserted during the daytime in mid-week, was as crowded as at train time on a Friday night. The dock was lined with boats, so that the two boys had to beach their canoes on the shore to one side. There was a small group of people talking on the dock and more on the station platform. As they passed the station door, Janet Morley came out and walked quietly away along the tracks toward the east. Ken saw from her eyes that she had been crying. Inside the station her father was busying himself with his duties.

On a bench at the far end of the station sat John Onaman, Henry Two Turtles and two men whom the boys had never seen before. Dressed in plain clothes, they might have been two businessmen who had stopped off at Kinniwabi on the way to their cottages. The four men sat staring at the ground. All were silent. Henry Two Turtles, a tall, slight youth with a badly pockmarked face, stood up and walked to the edge of the platform as the boys approached. Neither of the two detectives so much as glanced at him.

John Onaman looked up as the boys walked past. There was no sign of emotion, only resignation, on his face, but he summoned a bright smile of recognition. Ken and Paul stood there awkwardly for a moment and then went across the tracks to the store.

It was crowded inside and a heated discussion was going

on as the two boys entered. No one was buying anything and the atmosphere was more that of a meeting hall than of a store. All those in attendance were men, and they were ranged along the counters, on a bench beside the fire and against the back wall of the store.

Mr. Simpson was speaking as the boys came through the door.

". . . don't believe they did it," he said. "I don't believe it for a minute. I know those two boys, known them since they were babies, and I tell you right now that they never stole anything in their lives."

There was silence for a moment. It was apparent that there was a great amount of respect for the old storekeeper. But it was also clear that not everyone agreed with him.

"Well, I say leave it to the police," a voice spoke up. "After all, it's their business and they must know what they're doing."

"Yes, that's right," someone else agreed. "What do we know about it?"

Ben Simpson looked steadily at the speaker. His one eye, the one that had been injured long ago in an unknown accident, drooped strangely, but the other flashed through the gloom of the store.

"It could be," he said, "that we know a lot about it. At least I think I know Indians. There are good Indians and bad Indians, and John Onaman is one of the good ones. So is Henry Two Turtles."

"I, for one, agree with you," a voice from the back of the store said.

Ken turned to see Moose MacGregor sitting on the counter that served as the post office at Kinniwabi.

"You've got to know Indians to understand this thing," he said. "Mr. Simpson knows them better than I do—better than any man I know—but I know John Onaman, too. And I'd stake my life that he had nothing to do with these robberies."

Wilbur Crowe stepped out from the shadows at one side of the store. There was a condescending smile on his thick lips.

"Now, we all understand your sympathy with the Indians," he said. "You and Mr. Simpson, here, make your living from them, more or less. And you're their friends."

He made his last comment sound like an indictment.

"Some would say your sentiments are kind of noble, I suppose," he continued. "As for me, I don't object to your sticking up for them. Like I said to Mr. Morley just last night—I ain't one to hold a grudge against no man."

There was a smirk now in his voice as well as in the twisted corners of his mouth.

"But we have to face facts, don't we?"

"And just what," Moose MacGregor asked, "do you mean by that?"

Ken knew that Wilbur Crowe was enjoying this, liking the fact that he was the center of attention—liking, too, the fact that he could dominate this group of city people.

"Now, we all know you've got a soft spot in your heart for them Indians," he said. "Particularly livin' with them like you do. When you get too close to something, sometimes you can't see it right in front of your face."

"Get to the point, Wilbur," Ben Simpson said, his voice tight and carefully controlled.

"The point," Wilbur Crowe said, each word slow and

114

deliberate, "is that Indians are Indians. You and the ranger can think what you want to—that's your right—but the rest of us know that you can't trust any Indian. They'll steal your eyeteeth if you give them half a chance."

There was a long silence in the semidark room.

"Well," Moose MacGregor said, "that's better. At least we've got it all on the table now. Indians are Indians, eh Wilbur? They're all alike and they're all no good—that's what you're saying isn't it?"

"Maybe not exactly," Wilbur Crowe smirked, "but it's close enough. You can have all the fancy ideas you like, but everybody else in this room knows that that's the way it is. Maybe there's a good Indian somewhere—I just don't ever happen to have run across him, that's all."

There was a low murmur around the store. In part, Ken knew, it was a protest against the unfairness of Wilbur Crowe's statement. But in part, too, he admitted reluctantly to himself, it reflected some appreciation of his sneering humor and some willingness to concede that there "might be something in what he said."

Ken was very conscious of Paul's presence beside him. Paul was the only Indian in the store and, apart from John Onaman and Henry Two Turtles, the only one around the station. He wondered what his friend was thinking. A glance at Paul's face gave him no clue.

"If they didn't do it," Wilbur Crowe concluded, "who did? Do you want us to believe that somebody here in this room did it? Or somebody out there in the cottages?"

"Wait a minute," someone said from the front of the store. "We can go on talking and arguing about what we think forever, but it doesn't make much difference one way or the other, does it? The only thing that matters is the facts. What's the evidence against the Indians? Does anybody know?"

"That's the truth," Moose MacGregor agreed. "Even Wilbur Crowe here can't put a man in jail without evidence —even if he is an Indian."

"There's plenty of that, too," said Wilbur Crowe. "You don't have to take my word for it. Go talk to Mr. Morley up at the station."

"What evidence has he got?" someone asked.

"Ask him," Wilbur Crowe challenged.

"Yes," said Moose MacGregor, "yes, let's do that." He moved towards the door. "I'd like to hear it for myself."

The others followed him up the wooden walk towards the station, Ken and Paul tagging along at the end of the group. It seemed to Ken that most of the men felt vaguely uncomfortable—that, in this particular case, there was not so much strength in numbers, as embarrassment. They were used to leaving matters of this kind to the police and most of them resented their present involvement.

The station agent came to meet them at the door. As usual, his dress and grooming were impeccable.

"What's all this?" he asked.

"We thought maybe you'd tell us what you know about these robberies," Wilbur Crowe said. "Some of these gentlemen are asking for evidence and I told them that you might be able to oblige them."

"Evidence?" the station agent asked, his eyes narrowing behind his rimless glasses. "There isn't any shortage of that, is there? Seems to me that the case is open and shut. I wouldn't have thought anybody would have any doubts."

116

"Well, let's just say that some of us are a little stupid," Moose MacGregor said, "and not as sure as you are. How be you enlighten us some, eh?"

"All right. Suppose I told you that I saw them with my own eyes—would that convince you?"

Ken felt Paul tense beside him.

"Saw them doing what?" Mr. Simpson asked.

"I saw them not once, but twice," the station agent said. "On two different nights when cottages were broken into I saw them sneaking past the station here in the middle of the night. Quiet as animals, they were, and thought nobody saw them. But they were wrong. I saw them."

"Is that all?" Moose MacGregor asked. "Is there a law against walking past your station at night?"

"There's a law against what they were doing," the station agent said. "There's a law against breaking into decent peoples' cottages, isn't there?"

"Wait a minute," someone else said. "Just wait a minute now. Moose is right. The fact that you saw them doesn't prove anything. You've got to have more than that to go on."

"That's right," another voice added. "It's no crime to be out late at night. If it was, a lot of us would be in jail right now. Why, Irene and I were playing bridge over at the Andersons last night till after two. Why don't they arrest us, too?"

There was a murmur of assent.

Moose MacGregor walked over to where John Onaman and Henry Two Turtles sat on the station bench.

"John," he said, "what were you doing those nights when Morley saw you? I know there's an explanation. Tell us what it is."

John Onaman looked up at the forest ranger. He was obviously ill at ease under the stares of so many people and for a long moment Ken didn't think he was going to answer.

"Me and Henry were catching bullfrogs, Mr. Mac-Gregor," he said at last. "That's all. We were down in that marsh at the foot of the station bay. We often go there and catch frogs with a flashlight."

"Sure," Mr. Morley said, a sneer in his voice, "that's all you were doing—catching frogs. So why were you sneaking by here so quietly? Eh? Tell me that."

The young Indian did not look at the station agent, but continued to address his words to the big forest ranger.

"We weren't sneaking around," he said softly. "It was late and we just kept quiet so that we wouldn't wake everybody up—that's all."

The two detectives listened with bored disinterest. It was clear that they felt their duty was done. From here on it was somebody else's problem.

"Well, that satisfies me," Moose MacGregor said. "Is there any reason to doubt John's story? What could be more logical than that?"

"It doesn't satisfy me," Wilbur Crowe said. "They didn't want to wake everybody up! I can see them being worried about that when those dogs of theirs howl all night long and keep everybody from gettin' any sleep for miles around."

"What did you want with the bullfrogs?" someone else asked.

"Some of the big restaurants back home serve frogs' legs," another voice put in. "Did they ship any frogs to the city, Ben?"

"No, they didn't," said Mr. Simpson. "Not through me. But . . ."

"But nothing," Wilbur Crowe said. "What did you do with the frogs? Tell us that then."

Still John Onaman addressed himself to Moose MacGregor alone.

"We ate them."

"Well, now, isn't that something," D. R. Morley said scornfully. "These Indians served frogs' legs! Real gourmets! Imagine—frogs' legs! I hope you had the right wine to go with them."

"What's funny about eating frogs, Mr. MacGregor?" John Onaman asked.

"Frogs' legs are a luxury in the city," Moose MacGregor said quietly. "They're trying to say that you wouldn't be likely to eat a delicacy like frogs' legs."

"But I don't understand what they mean about frogs' legs," the young Indian said. "We often eat frogs. Frogs are good to eat—as good as turtles and better than snakes. Why wouldn't we eat frogs?"

"You mean you ate the whole frogs, don't you, John?" Moose MacGregor asked. "You ate them because they're good food. Not a delicacy, but a necessity."

He looked around the group, which had fallen suddenly quiet.

"You see," he said, "for the Ojibway it isn't easy to get meat. When you're an Indian, you eat what meat you can get."

The forest ranger suddenly dropped a hand on John Onaman's shoulder.

"I don't know about the rest of you," he said, "but I don't think much of the evidence so far." He looked straight at Wilbur Crowe. "I think you're going to have to do better than that," he said.

For a long moment Ken enjoyed a rekindling of hope. He sensed it in Paul, too, and in the two young prisoners sitting on the railway bench. And then, suddenly, it was shattered.

"What do you think of this for proof?" a new voice asked from the edge of the station platform. Ken turned to see Les Crowe and Dinnie Hackett. The latter stood with one hand in each hip pocket slouching a little, a contemptuous smile on his lips. Les Crowe, bulky beside his thin friend, held a rifle across his two outstretched arms.

"This is Mr. Roxborough's rifle, isn't it?" he asked. "At least it has his initials here on the butt."

"Let's see it," D. R. Morley said, moving towards the newcomers.

"No," said one of the detectives, rising and moving quickly in front of the station agent. "Let me see it."

He took the rifle from Les Crowe and examined it as the others crowded around. On the black butt, clear for all to see, were the initials W.H.R.—for William Henry Roxborough.

"Anybody recognize the rifle?" he asked.

"Yes, I know it," someone said. "I've hunted with Bill Roxborough for years and that's his gun."

"For sure?" asked the detective.

"Sure."

"Where did you find it, Les?" asked Wilbur Crowe.

"Maybe you'd better let us handle it," the detective said. "Okay, where?"

"Me and Dinnie found it," Les Crowe said. "We found it in his canoe." He indicated John Onaman with a wave of his hand.

"We figured they must have taken it and we went and looked in his canoe, that's all. And we found it there."

"You're willing to swear to that, the two of you?" asked the other detective.

"Sure we are—it's only the truth. Eh, Dinnie?"

"Yeah, Les, just the truth—that's all," Dinnie said in his oddly squeaky, high-pitched voice. "We found it there, sure enough."

"Then that about wraps it up," the detective with the rifle said. "Now maybe all you people had better go on home and leave the rest to us."

"Yeah, the train'll be through here in a half hour or so and we'll be on it," said the other detective. "The two of us and these boys here. And the sooner the better, as far as I'm concerned."

The group began to break up.

John Onaman looked up at Moose MacGregor.

"It's not true, Mr. MacGregor," he said. "What they said isn't true. We never took that rifle. And nobody found it in my canoe."

"I know," Moose MacGregor said. "I know, John. But for now there isn't much . . ."

The Indian boy turned away, his eyes dropping to the ground. He slumped on the railway bench as if the strength had suddenly left his body, and, in spite of his height and broad shoulders, he looked suddenly frail. Yet there was somehow the impression that he was not surprised by what had happened. In the silence they all heard the whistle of the westbound train from somewhere well down the line.

The station platform was now almost deserted.

Ken felt numb, helpless and intensely weary.

He turned to look at Paul, to see how his friend had reacted to what had happened.

Paul was gone. Ken's eyes searched the platform, the path

121

down to the dock, the tracks leading away from the station in both directions. There was no sign of his friend.

He turned, his heart heavy, and walked slowly down the hill to his canoe.

Chapter 14

As Ken reached the station dock he was surprised to see his mother and Aunt Marion just arriving in the motorboat. In the excitement of the arrests, he had forgotten that this was the day the two women were going into town. Their appearance in city clothes and with their suitcases snapped him back to the reality of everyday things.

"I'd forgotten that you were leaving," he said.

"No wonder," his mother said, "with all the turmoil going on over here. But don't forget to take care of things while we're gone. We'll be back with your father on the Friday night train."

He carried their bags up to the station and a few minutes later the train pulled in beside the platform. His mother and Aunt Marion got aboard while the conductor looked at his watch and the huge engine hissed impatiently down the track. Ken saw John Onaman, Henry Two Turtles and the detectives climb the steps of another car farther back in the train.

A few minutes later he pulled the bow of his canoe around the point and drifted to a stop beside the cottage dock. The look of the still fresh timbers reminded him of the work he had shared with Paul and Jacob Onaman—how long ago it suddenly seemed! It was strangely quiet at the cottage with everyone gone, and he found himself wandering aimlessly around, trying to settle down. He thought about going fishing, and even went so far as to put his gear into the canoe. But the idea had no real appeal. He sat in the living room, the quiet and emptiness around him an almost physical force, and finally turned on the transistor radio, but the music was depressing and the voice of the announcer so artificially gay that he soon switched it off. He had not eaten since breakfast, but he did not have the energy to bother with food.

Finally, with no purpose in mind, he wandered into his bedroom. He stood at the window looking out across the lake. In the late afternoon the shadows were beginning to steal out from the near shore across the lake. The sun danced on the gentle ripples. And once again he seemed to hear those whispering voices and the sound of a paddle scraping against a gunwale in the night. Whose was that high-pitched voice? If only he could remember.

He sat on the edge of his bed and idly picked up the box containing the photography outfit he had received for his birthday. He thought about some of the pictures he could take that winter at home—basketball games, Christmas, winter scenes. And as he thought about these things an idea suddenly came to him. It was a vagrant, ill-defined thought at first, but as he sat there the outlines of it gradually began to take shape in his mind.

I wonder if it might work, he thought. It's a crazy idea—a one-in-a-hundred chance—but, well, it was better than nothing. If they set it up just right and if they had a great deal of luck, who knew, maybe it just might come off. Wait a minute, now, let's go over it again. He went through it, step by step, in his mind. As he filled out the details, a faint excitement came over him—the first ray of sunlight in the gloom of that unhappy day.

After a while he left the cottage and hurried down to his canoe. The sun was beginning to drop towards the west and the lake was still and quiet. The scene was so familiar and yet, after the events of the day, it seemed somehow alien and unfriendly. He worked his paddle hard, pushing the canoe as rapidly as possible towards the Indian village.

The evening fires were lit now and several columns of smoke drifted almost straight up in the quiet air. A dog barked as he drew his canoe up on the beach, but otherwise no attention was paid to him.

This time there was no mistaking the hostility of the Ojibway. As he walked among the dwellings he saw no single human being. Everyone was inside. The village seemed deserted.

He made his way straight to the Onaman's house. There was no answer to his knock, and after three unsuccessful attempts he called out softly.

"Paul," he called, "Paul, it's me, Ken. Please let me talk to you."

Again there was no answer. He called again, and again.

"Listen, Paul, I want to help. I've got an idea, but I need to talk it over with you. Please come to the door."

Still the unopened door mocked him.

"Paul, come on. Open the door, for pete's sake. If you won't help me, who will?"

There was another long moment's silence and then the door swung slowly open. It did not open all the way and Ken could see Paul only dimly in the semidarkness inside.

"Come on out a minute, Paul," he said softly. "I think I know something that might work. Let me at least tell you about it."

For another few seconds Paul looked at him through solemn, not entirely trusting, brown eyes. And then the door swung wide and Paul stepped out.

"Let's go down by the lake and talk," Ken said.

Paul did not speak, but followed him down the path. They sat side by side on an old pine log at the edge of the beach. Ken talked at length about his idea, filling in the details he had already worked out and leaving the balance for later discussion if Paul accepted his basic plan.

The Indian boy listened without making any kind of reply. His eyes showed a flicker of interest as Ken went on, but he made no comment and asked no questions until Ken finished.

Even then he sat silently for another long moment.

"Do you think it might work?" he asked finally.

"It's a long shot," Ken said, "but it's at least a chance. I'm ready to try anything, aren't you?"

"Yes, it might work," Paul said thoughtfully. "We know whoever did it is still free, and if they're greedy enough they might try again. How do we set the bait?"

They talked on at length. Ken was delighted that he had imparted some of his enthusiasm to his friend—anything was better than the terrible apathy he had seen in his eyes earlier that day. They gradually worked out the details of the plan. At last they were finished.

"It's crazy," Paul said.

"It's absurd," Ken said. "Just ridiculous."

They laughed suddenly, together.

"But it's all we have," said Ken.

"So," Paul said, "let's give it a try, anyway."

"We'll make it work," Ken said. "Now then, the first

thing is to put out the bait. I'll go over to the station and make as much noise as I can. I just hope lots of people are around to hear it—especially the right people, whoever they are."

"Then later on, after dark, I'll come over to your place," Paul said. "I'll come as quietly as I can and I'll pull the canoe up in that little bay around the point from your cottage."

"Then we're all set for now," Ken said. "I'll be on my way and I'll see you later."

He started to get into his canoe and then, on an impulse, turned and shook hands with his friend.

"Lots of luck," he said.

"You, too," said Paul. "We'll need it."

Ken paddled down to the station. The sun was low in the west now and the lake like a mirror. As he paddled along the shore, two ducks flew over his head, their wings whistling. A loon called down in the bay and another answered from far up the lake. There was some hope now, however meager, and it was once again the Kinniwabi he knew.

He was pleased to see that there were several boats at the station dock. Good. The bigger the audience, the better chance that his words might fall on the proper ears.

He went on up to the store. There was quite a crowd inside and Mr. and Mrs. Simpson were looking after several people at once. Others were standing around, waiting their turns and talking over the events of the day. Ken saw Moose MacGregor standing toward the back, talking to one of the railway section hands. Mr. Palmer, the secretary of the Cottagers' Association, was there with his wife and their small children. He spotted several other cottagers whom he knew

127

by name. Wilbur Crowe was sitting on the back counter. Les Crowe and Dinnie Hackett stood nearby.

Ken waited for a few minutes and then decided it was time to play his part.

"Mr. Simpson," he said, "I'm sorry to interrupt, but I want to get back to the cottage before dark. Everybody but me has gone into the city and I have to tow my canoe over behind the motorboat. Could I just ask you something and then I'll be on my way?"

"Sure, I guess so, Ken," the storekeeper said. "These folks won't mind waiting a minute or two, will you?"

The customer whom Mr. Simpson had been waiting on shook his head and told Ken to go ahead.

"Thanks. Well, as I say everybody else has gone to town for a few days." He made his voice as loud as he dared without having it sound too unnatural. "Our new motor is acting up and my dad wants me to send it into the city for repairs. I've got to use it to get the boat back and tow the canoe. Otherwise I'd leave it here."

He glanced around the store to see how much attention was being paid to what he was saying. One or two had probably overheard but the rest seemed disquietingly unaware of the conversation.

"If I put it back in the crate and nailed it up," he continued doggedly, "could you arrange to have somebody pick it up and bring it over to the station?"

He watched Mr. Simpson's eyes carefully, seeing the surprise registered there. This was a critical moment because only a couple of days earlier Mr. Warren had told the storekeeper that the new motor was "running like a watch."

"I'm sorry to bother you about it," Ken said, "but it'll be too heavy for me to handle with the crate and all."

Mr. Simpson still had a question mark in his eyes and Ken decided to risk giving him a sign. He just hoped that the old man was shrewd enough to pick it up.

"There isn't any hurry," he said, winking as he spoke. "I'll just leave it on the dock for you to pick up whenever you can make arrangements."

To his relief he saw a flash of understanding pass over the old man's face. His one sound eye blinked ever so slightly.

"That'll be all right, Ken," he said. "I'm sure I can find somebody around here who will pick it up for you. It might take a day or two, though, before I can make arrangements."

Ken went out and down towards the dock. He did not know how well the first part of the plan had gone, but he had done his best. All we can do, he thought, is cross our fingers.

He tied the canoe behind the motorboat and pushed away from the dock. Just in case anyone was watching, he surreptitiously turned the throttle on the steering handle to the stop position two or three times. To an observer it would have seemed that the motor had suddenly cut out on him. Each time it stopped he pulled the starting cord several times, with the throttle still turned to the off position. He tried to make it appear that he was tinkering with the controls in an effort to make it start. He knew that it was unlikely that he had an audience, but he was determined to play it all the way.

Finally he let the motor settle into its normal smooth rhythm and proceeded on his slow, steady way across the lake. The sun was touching the treetops as he turned the point and headed into the dock. It would be dark in another half-hour.

He tied both boats up and then went to work to unhitch

the motor. Moments later he set it on its side on top of the dock and went up to the boathouse for its crate. A few minutes work with the hammer completed the job. Well, he thought, standing back, at least the trap is baited. I wonder what it will catch?

He went back up to the cottage. Under the trees it was almost full night now and he had to grope his way up the familiar path. He lit a lamp in the kitchen and started a fire in the cook stove. He had not eaten much all day—how long ago breakfast seemed!—and he was suddenly very hungry. He put some bacon in the frying pan and found a tin of pork and beans in the cupboard. The warmth of the fire and the crackle of the frying bacon were good and the light from the coal oil lamp was friendly and comforting.

While the food was cooking, he got his camera from the bedroom. There was a new film in it. He put a bulb in the holder, making certain that it was tight enough to ensure contact when the shutter lever was pushed down. He put several more bulbs beside the camera, checked that the film was set ready for the first exposure, and then, satisfied with his arrangements, he set a place for himself at the kitchen table, filled his plate from the stove and began to eat.

The odds were about a thousand to one against them—or maybe a million to one. What they needed was a miracle.

But he thought, taking a last forkful of beans from his plate, any long shot was better than no chance at all.

Chapter 15

He had just finished drying his dishes and was putting them away, when he heard a whispered call through the screen of the kitchen window.

"Ken, it's me, Paul."

Ken was a little startled. He had heard no sound before that to warn of Paul's arrival, although the night was very still and quiet.

"Good," he said. "I'll let you in."

"No, no," the whisper came back. "I'll stay here in the dark until you're ready. In case anyone is watching, it would be better if they don't know I'm here."

Ken smiled to himself. Paul was carrying on in the same vein as his playacting with the motor. He was right, too. It was better to overlook no detail.

"Okay," he said quietly. "I'll be with you in a minute. Let me just put these plates in the cupboard."

He blew out the light in the kitchen, picked up the camera and bulbs and stepped out into the darkness, being careful not to let the screen door slam.

It was pitch dark, and Paul was only a vague movement in the shadows as the two boys went down the path to the boathouse. But just as they reached it, an almost full moon broke through the clouds and bathed them in ghostly white light.

Paul's hand pulled Ken close against the boathouse wall.

131

"Let's wait here a second," he whispered. "The moon will go in again soon and then we can take our places."

Ken watched the night sky. While the moon was out he could see details around them almost as clearly as if it had been daytime. The crated motor on the dock stood out clearly. In a few seconds the clouds, drifting gently across the night sky, edged in front of the moon again.

"Okay," he said, "let's go."

Moving as quietly as they could in the darkness, they edged over toward the dock. A few feet to one side of it a stand of young willows grew at the water's edge.

"This should do," Paul whispered.

Groping with their hands they found enough room to sit down, facing the lake and reasonably well hidden should the moon break through again. Ken pulled a piece of driftwood and some small stones from beneath him and tossed them aside.

"Might as well get comfortable," he whispered. "We may be in for a long wait."

"Do you think they'll come?" Paul asked. "Did you make sure lots of people heard you over at the store?"

"I don't know, Paul. I made it as clear as I could without tipping our hand. And Mr. Simpson helped, too. He sure is sharp. Caught on right away. But whether the right people heard it or not, who can say?"

They fell silent then, each pursuing his own thoughts and listening to the varied sounds of the summer night. From far around the lake they heard the monotonous yet strangely melodic chorus of bullfrogs, and Ken remembered John Onaman's explanation of what he and Henry Two Turtles had been doing those other nights. Every now and then a fish jumped out in the lake and Ken helped pass the time by trying to guess its kind and size. A pike, he would say to himself. Big one—maybe ten pounds; or again, a small bass over by Hendren's Point. A whippoorwill was active for a while but then moved away out of hearing range. Occasionally they heard movements back in the bush. For the most part these sounded like small animals, rabbits perhaps, or raccoons, but once Ken thought he could hear a deer moving around behind the boathouse.

Time dragged slowly on. The moon burst through spasmodically during the first hour and then, as the clouds cleared away, it came out to stay. Its path was wide and silvery across the still lake and its light so bright that the reflections from the shore were almost as sharp as in daylight.

They both heard a train whistle far down the track to the west and listened as it came on towards Kinniwabi. Ken heard it whistle for Bradley's Bay, then, a few minutes later and closer now, for Otter Lake. Finally, they could make out the rumble of its engines and they watched its glaring headlight as it chugged ponderously around the long curve past the station. A long freight. Its noise filled the night for a few minutes and then it was gone, its whistle receding gradually into the east.

Around the lake the lights of the cottages began to blink out. Finally they were all gone except for one at the Robinson place on the far shore. Mr. Robinson must be reading an interesting book, Ken thought, or maybe one of the children is ill. But then that light, too, was gone and there was only the moon across the water.

The boys grew more uncomfortable as the hours dragged slowly by. The rock Ken was sitting on had seemed smooth enough at first—almost like a chair, he had thought. But as time passed he came to realize that the rock had sharp bumps. Barely noticeable early in the night, they came to seem like nails by the time midnight passed. Their legs grew cramped and they were both aware of an unsuspected chill edge on the night air.

Still nothing happened. The moon swung slowly across the sky, but no boat crossed its path. The motor was still conspicuous on the dock, but no hand reached out of the night for it.

"Not so good, eh?" Paul whispered at last.

"Uh, uh," Ken said, trying to keep discouragement from his voice. "But the night I heard those voices it was later than this, I think. It must have been after two o'clock."

"Can't be far from that now," Paul said.

They lapsed again into silence and, as the night matured, they both found that they had to fight against a tendency to drift off into sleep.

Ken forced his mind to concentrate on specific problems. If the trap worked (if John and Henry were not guilty) who would come to their bait? Whose voice had it been that he had heard that other night? The high-pitched whisper—who did it belong to? Who? Who? Who? Oh, come on, he thought, concentrate. You know that voice. Who owns it? Who? Who? Who?

He jerked himself back from the edge of sleep and moved slightly to ease the aches in his stiff muscles. I guess, he thought, this is a crazy scheme, a wild, hopeless gamble taken out of desperation. Probably no one was coming. Probably no one had heard his carefully planned dialogue except a few bored cottagers. Perhaps they should call it a night and go to bed. Maybe John Onaman and Henry Two Turtles did do it after all . . . wait, what was that?

He realized then that he had been subconsciously aware of vague sounds in the bush for several minutes. He had dismissed them as signaling the return of the deer he had heard earlier. But these were not the movements of a deer. A deer is light and quick, even in darkness. The foot that just snapped that twig was ponderous and awkward.

Ken nudged Paul, but realized from his friend's tenseness that he, too, had heard the movements behind them. For a long moment there was silence and then he heard another sound—a whispered curse as someone tripped over an unseen deadfall.

The moonlight, he thought, that's it—the moonlight. He and Paul had assumed all along that the thieves would come, if they came at all, by canoe. That would have been the easiest way and the fastest. But, because of the bright moonlight, they had decided to come through the bush. They had no doubt pulled their canoe up in the bushes somewhere around the point.

Now he and Paul were in potential trouble because the thieves would have to go past them only a few feet away to reach the dock.

"Still," Paul whispered, his lips tight against Ken's ear.

The two boys froze where they were, fighting off their fatigue and stiffness and struggling to control their excitement. Ken was afraid even to turn his head, but by straining his eyes he could just see the near end of the boathouse.

Another tense minute passed, and another. Now the sounds were just behind the boathouse. And then, suddenly, Ken heard the same whispered voice of that other, earlier night.

"Better wait here a minute," the muffled, but high-pitched, voice said, "till that moon's gone in."

He was too tense to concentrate but the voice was again familiar. And again it defied identification.

An instant later the bright path of the moon across the water was rolled up as the clouds again moved over the sky. The sudden darkness was almost absolute.

Then there was a sound of movement beside them and not more than ten feet away. They could sense someone moving carefully along the dock, but their probing eyes could not detect even the vaguest of silhouettes. They would have to guess when to make their move. Ken's fingers tightened around the camera. He felt desperately for the shutter lever that would set off the flash bulb and take the picture. There it was. Now, steady. Don't panic. He hoped that his stiff and weak legs would hold him when the time came.

Now his eyes were adjusting a little to the darkness. Strange, he thought, it's never completely dark even when there is no moon and no stars.

"Here it is," a voice whispered—another voice, not the high-pitched whisper this time, but deeper and stronger.

"Wait a minute," said the high-pitched whisper. "Wait till I get ahold of it."

There were the sounds of further movement and some muffled curses.

"Must weigh a ton," a whisper said.

"Never mind—just grab it."

Another long pause and more muttered curses followed.

"Hurry up."

"Okay, okay. I've got it."

Ken nudged Paul lightly. It won't be long now, he thought. I hope, I hope I don't make a mess of it. There will be just one chance. Don't let me fumble it.

Suddenly Paul squeezed his shoulder lightly and Ken knew that his friend, too, had his fingers crossed.

"Wait a minute," the high-pitched whisper said. "Put it down. I haven't got a good hold on it."

"C'mon, c'mon," the other voice whispered. "We ain't got all night. Let's go before the kid hears us."

"All right, do you want to carry it yourself?"

There was another long pause. They heard the crate scraping on the dock and there were more muttered exclamations.

"I wish the moon would come out. I can't see a thing."

"Sure," said the other voice, growing steadily more impatient. "Maybe we should turn on the flashlight. Hurry up, for heaven's sake. There's still a light on at the cottage."

Oh, oh, Ken thought, that was stupid. He had forgotten to turn out the lamp in the cottage living room. That could have killed the whole plan. They were lucky that the two men on the dock had decided to take a chance.

"Oh, what difference does that make?" the high-pitched voice asked. "The kid's probably afraid to sleep in the dark."

"Never mind what he's afraid of," the other voice said. "Grab that thing and we'll get out of here."

"Okay, I got it. Let's go."

They heard the two men moving toward them along the dock. Ken's fingers tightened on the camera and he braced one foot against a rock for better purchase when the time came to move. Steady now, steady. The camera manual said that the subjects should be within ten or twelve feet for best results. That would be just about the time the two of them stepped from the dock onto the shore. Wait. Steady.

He gave Paul a light nudge in the ribs with his elbow, and in the same instant pushed himself to his feet. He sensed Paul jumping up beside him as he swung the camera to his eye. There would be no chance to take any sighting in that pitch darkness; he would have to focus the camera by judgment alone. There, that should do it. Don't move the camera. Now!

He pushed the small lever down firmly, careful to keep the camera steady. A flash of astonishing brilliance lit up the area in front of them. Ken's eyes were momentarily blinded by the sudden glare, but in the first instant after he pressed the lever he saw two men at the edge of the dock, no more than eight feet from him. They were bent over, struggling under the weight of the crated outboard motor.

There was only a split second before the stygian blackness closed over them again, but in that instant Ken recognized the two men. And, in that pinpoint of time, before he was forced to think of his next move, he finally knew who owned the high-pitched voice. Dinnie Hackett. And the other man, crouched under the weight of their burden, was Les Crowe.

In the brief flash Ken saw the look of startled surprise in their eyes and heard a curse of astonishment.

"What the—," Les Crowe began.

And then Ken felt Paul's hand pulling demandingly at his arm.

"Come on, Ken. Come on. Out of here."

Ken suddenly realized that he had not figured out what to do after the picture was taken. His mind had been so filled with the question of success or failure in getting the evidence they needed that he had never contemplated what to do once they had it. Somehow he knew that Paul would take over at this point. He did not think this consciously, but merely accepted it. He had done his part in getting the picture. Now it would be up to Paul to get them out of there so that they could make use of it.

Paul took his arm more firmly and pulled him almost savagely. It was none too soon. Behind them Ken heard a quick movement, and he felt strong fingers just slip off his shoulder. The lunge carried his attacker into the bushes.

Ken felt himself almost dragged the first few feet. Then he was running on his own, running wildly, desperately, through the black night.

"Hold onto my shirt," Paul whispered. "Hold on tight and let me lead the way."

He could hear the two men behind them, all idea of secrecy gone now, charging after them through the bush. He clung desperately to the camera with one hand and held a thick handful of Paul's shirt with the other. They went straight back from the boathouse into the woods away from the lake.

Berry bushes tore at his trousers and scratched his face and arms. Fallen trees, unseen, tore the skin off his shins. Rocks tripped him. His desperate feet slipped and betrayed him, but still he stumbled on—half running, half dragged along by the unseen figure of his friend in front of him.

Once he fell and a rock dug into his ribs, tearing the breath away from him. He did not think he could get up and go on, but Paul put a hand under his arm and pulled him to his feet.

"Come on, Ken," he said. "Come on. You can do it."

He made himself hurry on into the chaotic darkness, away from the noises of pursuit behind them.

Chapter 16

On and on they plunged through the black forest. After a while Ken lost all track of time. It seemed then that this wild flight had begun somewhere far back in the mists of time, and that it might continue infinitely into the future.

He was sore, now, all over. Perspiration ran down his face and stung his eyes. His chest ached. His feet no longer seemed to belong to him. He was scratched and torn and bruised. Repeatedly he tripped and fell and each time it took a greater act of will to drag himself to his feet again.

Paul seemed to have some kind of sixth sense. He tripped and stumbled occasionally, but never completely lost his footing. Ken did not know how he avoided running straight into a tree in the blackness, but somehow the Ojibway found his way through them.

They could not elude their pursuers. Sometimes the sound of pursuit was close on their heels; sometimes it receded enough to raise their hopes. But each time they stopped to fight for breath, they knew that Dinnie and Les were coming on relentlessly behind them.

Suddenly Paul stopped, his hand tightening on Ken's shoulder. Ken obediently froze in his tracks. Then Paul was dragging him down to the ground.

"What the . . . ?" he began.

"Shhh," Paul said. "The moon—it's coming out again."

Ken glanced upwards through a gap in the trees. It was true. The moon was vaguely visible through thinning clouds. In an instant it would burst out into a patch of clear sky.

"In there," Paul said, pushing Ken towards a grove of cedars. "Quick."

They scrambled through the closely woven branches, squirming to get as deeply into the thicket as possible. They were just in time. An instant later the moon flooded the forest with light. The boys lay still, afraid almost to breathe.

"All right," a voice said harshly. "Careful now, Dinnie. They got to be right here some place."

Ken could see two figures working their way gradually towards their hiding place. Both were bent low, heads turning from side to side, eyes peering for some sign of the two boys. Step by step they worked their way nearer to the cedar thicket.

"C'mon, Ken," Paul whispered. "We've got to get out of here. *Niguim*—hurry."

The boys crawled out the far side of the protecting cedars, worming their way over the uneven ground on their stomachs. A broken branch dug into Ken's ribs and he bit his lip to hold back a cry of pain. They worked their way slowly along in that fashion for some fifty feet. Then Paul eased himself to his feet.

"Let's make a break for it," he said in a low voice. "It's our only chance."

They dashed into the forest, running faster now by the light of the moon. The short pause had restored them a little and they ran wildly, desperately. It seemed for a moment as if they might shake off their pursuers by that sudden spurt.

But then Ken caught his foot in an unseen crevice. Just to his left was a steep rock facing, a sheer drop of about eight

141

feet. He danced insanely for an instant on the brink of it, trying desperately to regain his balance. And then in stubborn surrender to the inevitable triumph of gravity, he slowly tottered over the edge. He landed on the hard ground below with a sickening thud, his fall broken only slightly by some juniper bushes at the base of the rock. The breath went completely out of his body and a new kind of blackness closed over him. For a split second he lost consciousness.

Then Paul jumped down beside him.

"Ken," he asked, his voice worried, "are you all right?"

"I don't know," Ken said, gasping for breath against the pain. "I don't know."

"Did you break anything, do you think?"

The pain subsided gradually and in a few seconds he was able to pull himself to his knees. He groped around in the semidarkness until his fingers found the camera. It seemed certain that it must be broken, but he hoped that some miracle had protected it. They were in a natural depression some thirty feet across. The rock facing ran around three sides of it, straight and sheer like the walls of a swimming pool. On the fourth side the way was partially blocked by thick raspberry bushes. It was to all intents and purposes a trap. Paul's eyes searched desperately for a way out as Ken pulled himself painfully to his feet. He ached all over, but he could stand.

Then the figures of Les Crowe and Dinnie Hackett appeared again in the moonlight, this time at the top of the rock wall.

"There they are," Dinnie Hackett shouted.

"Yeah," Les Crowe said, "and this time they won't get away. Move around that side, and I'll go this way."

"Watch it," Dinnie said, "the moon's gonna go again."

"All right, all right. Won't do them no good."

Then the moon was gone again, the darkness closing in more deeply now after the moonlight.

"Listen careful," Les Crowe said. "Listen for 'em to move."

"This way," Paul whispered, his lips hard against Ken's ear. "Follow me, but be as quiet as you can."

Paul moved slowly across the bare ground of the depression, towards the berry bushes. Ken followed, lips tight against the pain, wondering what plan he had in mind.

When they reached the far side, Paul stopped him.

"When this tree goes, we go—back up the wall where you fell," he whispered.

Ken saw the dim outline of a dead tree, a half-rotten poplar about six inches through the trunk, just in front of Paul. Now that they were closer Ken sensed that the ground fell away behind the berry bushes, although he couldn't be sure in the darkness. Paul must have noted these things, he realized, in the brief time that the moon had been out.

"Okay," Paul whispered, "here goes. Help me push."

They took hold of the dead tree, put their shoulders to it and shoved with all their combined might. For a discouraging instant the tree would not give.

"Hard," Paul whispered. "All you've got."

Ken tensed himself again, bracing one foot behind him, and drove into the tree like a football player practicing on a blocking dummy.

Suddenly the tree relinquished its tenuous hold on the earth and began to fall. Ken and Paul had to. shift their weight quickly to avoid following it. The tree went crashing through the berry bushes and then bounced noisily down the slope away from them. It continued its wild plunge for several seconds, but long before it came to a stop, Ken and Paul were on their way.

Paul led the way. He seemed to sense exactly how far it was through the darkness to the rock wall. A quick leap took him halfway up and his groping fingers found a hold on a root at the upper edge. In an instant he was at the top, reaching down to give Ken a hand. A strong pull and a lucky foothold in the rock, and Ken scrambled up beside him.

"Good," said Paul, "now let's get out of here."

They hurried away once more into the darkness. At first they had no idea whether or not Paul's trick had worked, but as the minutes passed and they heard no pursuit, hope began to grow. Ken's body was still racked with pain from the fall, but it was gradually abating.

Twenty minutes later, Paul stopped, his hand tightening on Ken's arm.

"I think we've done it," he said. "Haven't heard anything for a long while. Let's rest a minute."

They lay down on the crest of a ridge on the moss between the rocks. The moon was now a hazy ball behind thin clouds. Overhead the sky had changed from a pattern of broken clouds to unrelieved overcast. It was evident that the moon would neither come out full again that night nor completely disappear. In its pale light it was possible to make out vague outlines.

Paul pointed to the low ground in front of the ridge.

"That's Jackson's swamp down there," he said. "It's about a half mile wide and there's a small creek in the middle of it. It would be tough to cross at night, but if we could get through it we'd have an easy walk to the railway track."

"How far?"

"Maybe a mile the other side of the swamp."

"Is that the best way?" Ken asked.

"The only way," Paul said. "We can't go back or they'll find us. Can't go that way because of the lake. And to the east there's nothing but bush for a hundred miles."

"Okay, let's go."

His friend was silent for a second.

"It'll be tough," he said. "Real tough. The swamp's slimy and full of holes. And there'll be a million mosquitoes."

"I bet there will," Ken said. "But you're the boss. Let's go."

They worked their way down the gradual slope from the ridge. It was treacherous in the half light, but the vegetation was sparse and they made good time. After a while the way was disarmingly easy. The thick moss seemed almost like a carpet after the rough, hard trail over the rocks. But after a while water began to ooze up under their feet. Soon it had crept up to their ankles and then halfway to their knees.

Each step became more laborious as the mud and water sucked at their feet and the spongy muskeg gave under their weight. Then the mosquitoes were on them.

Ken had been before where the mosquitoes were bad at Kinniwabi, but he had never seen anything like what they encountered in the next few minutes. The insects came as a solid cloud around them, getting in their eyes, their ears, their hair, almost choking away their breath. Hysteria swept over Ken. It didn't build gradually, but seized him suddenly in the first few minutes. I'll go mad, he thought. I can't go on. I'll die here.

"Ken," Paul was shouting at him, "take some mud. Ken,

listen to me. Take some mud like this. Smear it all over your face. Hurry, Ken! Now! Now! Do it now!"

Ken made himself follow his friend's command. He reached under the water and lifted two handfuls of thick, black mud. He smeared it on his face, into his hair, down his neck. In a few seconds he felt it begin to dry on his skin. The mosquitoes did not go away and they did not break off their attack. But, though they buzzed around still in their infinite numbers, only a comparative few landed on his skin. The mud was in his eyes and in his mouth and up to his nose, but the partial relief from the mosquitoes restored a measure of calm and snatched him back from the brink of insanity.

"Okay?" Paul asked. "Can you go on now?"

"Yes," Ken said weakly, "I think so. Let's give it a try."

They moved ahead through the gradually deepening swamp. Ken forced his mind to concentrate on the task of placing one foot in front of the other. Left, right, left, right. Lift it up. Push it forward. Put it down. Now drag the other foot from the muck. Lift it. Push it forward. Put it down.

"We're doing fine," Paul said after a while. "We're nearly halfway there. Just be glad there are no crocodiles or poisonous snakes to worry about."

"I am glad," Ken said, "but I wish you hadn't mentioned snakes."

After a while they came to the creek.

"There's the end of the swamp over there," Paul said, pointing. "You can see the trees in the moonlight. This little creek is nothing—only fifteen or twenty feet wide."

"How deep is it?" Ken asked.

"Deep enough—over our heads in the middle—but there isn't much current. It'll cool us off."

They pushed out into the water, feeling it rise to their knees and then slowly up along their bodies. Suddenly the ground dropped away under Ken's feet, and he struck out, kicking with his feet and pulling strongly with one arm as he held the camera out of the water with the other. The water made the cuts and scratches on his body smart, but the swim was quickly over and they pulled themselves out on the far bank.

"More mud," Paul said, and they repeated the process of smearing their exposed skin.

They listened for sounds of pursuit but the swamp behind them was as quiet as it was black.

"Nothing to it now," Paul said. "Just up over that rise in front of us, and the tracks are in sight."

Ken wondered how much more his body would take. He thought about this in a curiously disinterested way, as if it had nothing really to do with him—as if his body somehow belonged to someone else. That is an interesting line of thought, he said to himself, if only I weren't too tired to pursue it further.

Paul led the way again and after a few more minutes the swamp began to recede under their feet and they gradually progressed onto firmer ground. Walking became steadily easier. I'm getting my second wind, Ken thought—or is it my third or tenth?

Soon they entered the forest once more. It was easier now that they could take time to pick their way and after a few minutes Paul found a deer run that led in the direction they wanted. Ken suddenly wondered what time it might be. It seemed like days since they had snapped that flash picture back at the cottage. He knew it could not be very long before dawn.

He watched the dim outlines of his friend moving steadily ahead of him through the gloom. The young Ojibway looked as fresh and strong as when they had started this wild flight. Is he completely impervious to hardship, Ken wondered? Doesn't he feel anything? Is he immune to fatigue and pain? He thought these things not with resentment but with a vast incredulity.

After a while Paul held up a hand to stop.

"Do you hear anything—off that way? I thought I could hear the engine of a train."

Just then a train whistle came to them through the night. It was quite close, not as close as Kinniwabi, but probably at Crowe Falls just down the line.

They waited there listening for further sounds of the train. It whistled again a few moments later and then Ken, too, could hear the rising whine of a diesel engine as it struggled up a grade.

"How far away do you think the track is?" he asked.

"Don't know, exactly," Paul answered. "It's hard to tell in the darkness, but I wouldn't think it's far now. We should know in a minute."

The sound of the train grew nearer and nearer, and a few seconds later they saw brief flashes of its headlight through the trees just ahead. They were almost on top of the railway track, and the roar and rumble of the train shut out everything else as it hurtled by just ahead of them. As it gradually died away in the east, the stillness of the night closed in once more.

A few more yards through the trees and their feet

crunched on the gravel and cinders of the roadbed. It was an incredible relief to walk on level, firm footing.

"Let's take a rest for a minute," Ken suggested, "before we start out for the station."

They sank down on some railway ties piled beside the track. I'll be lucky if I ever get up again, Ken thought. The pain in his body had given way to an overpowering weariness. He looked at Paul, relaxed and apparently fresh, beside him.

"I don't know how you do it," he said. "I'm about to die and you look like you could go on forever."

Paul smiled in the thin light.

"What makes you think that?" Paul asked.

"Just the way you look. I'm jealous, I guess. To know how I feel and then to think it just rolls off your back . . ."

Paul laughed quietly.

"That is funny," he said. "Why do you think I am not tired, my friend? Do I not have a heart like yours, and lungs like yours, and muscles like yours? Don't the bushes scratch me as they do you? Doesn't my skin bruise as yours does?"

Ken looked closely at his friend.

"I know that you must be tired," he said, "but you'd never tell it from looking at you. Me, I wish I could just go to bed and stay there for a month, that's all."

"Don't be fooled, Ken," Paul said quietly. "I know that in a moment we must get up and start for the station, and right now I am quite sure I won't be able to do it. I am so tired I can't feel anything. Just like you."

He paused for a moment.

"But the deer is tired when he is chased by the wolves. And the fish is tired when he fights against the hook. It is natural to be tired and there is nothing to be done about it. Only now I am tired as I have never been before."

Ken put his hand lightly on his friend's shoulder.

"Okay," he said, "maybe it will kill us both to move. But we still have some things to do. So let's go—at least we'll die together."

Chapter 17

At first the roadbed of the railway seemed as smooth as a paved street after the long struggle through the forest and swamp. But after a while the ties began to seem higher and more inconsistently spaced with each step. For a while Ken concentrated on spreading his steps so that he would tread on two consecutive ties and then skip one. But he was too tired to maintain this pattern and soon he was content merely to stumble along, letting his feet fall when they might.

He kept watching the eastern sky for signs of dawn. Once there was a long, lighter streak across the horizon, but it closed over again. Maybe that was the so-called false dawn I've heard about, Ken thought. It seemed blacker than ever now. What do they say—that it's darkest just before the dawn?

On and on they walked like automatons, close to the edge of collapse, virtually asleep on their feet. It was because of their near-exhaustion that they failed to hear the train. The late night was perfectly still and ordinarily they would have heard a whistle or two of warning from well down the track. But in their struggle to keep going, they had both concentrated all their attention on putting one foot before the other.

They were walking through a rock cut, perhaps a hundred yards long and eight or ten feet from track bed to crest. The cut had been blasted out of solid granite and the walls were jagged and perpendicular. It was a narrow cut, the sheer walls rising only a few feet from the ends of the ties on either side.

They heard the train for the first time, only a mere instant before they saw its headlight. One minute there was silence; the next, the night was filled with the roar of the engine, the grinding squeal of the wheels on the curve. The ties and rails vibrated beneath them. The headlight plunged into the cut and seemed to envelope the whole world in its brilliance.

The boys were some two-thirds of the way through when the train suddenly descended upon them. In the first instant they both stood there as though paralyzed. Then Paul grabbed Ken by the arm and pulled him from the tracks and against the rock facing. Ken crashed violently against the wall and the air was once more driven from his lungs. They pressed their backs tight to the rock and in an instant the engine was upon them.

In that split second, they both saw something that greatly increased their sense of peril. The jabbing beam of the head-light showed them two other figures against the rock on the other side and toward the far end of the cut. Les Crowe and Dinnie Hackett. So sure were they that they had made good their escape, that they had almost forgotten their pursuers. It seemed impossible that they were once again threatened, but there was no denying what their eyes had seen.

The train was a long, fast freight. The cars plunged and rumbled by them in what seemed an endless chain—box-cars, flatcars, coal cars, undulating in a staccato dance of power. The noise in that confined space was overpowering. The suction of the train's passing tried to pull them away from the rock and drag them under the wheels. Dust swirled and got into their mouths and nostrils and eyes.

Then Ken felt a tug on his arm. Paul was pulling desperately at him and pointing upwards with his other hand. What was he trying to say? Surely you don't mean that we're going to climb that rock wall, he thought. That's impossible. We'll both fall and be cut to pieces under the train. But Paul kept on gesturing, and a second later turned and began to crawl upwards. His progress was desperately slow as his fingers groped for crevice or protrusion and his feet sought toeholds in the inhospitable rock. He looked clumsy and his frantic efforts seemed futile. Yet gradually, foot by foot, he wormed his way up toward the top.

Ken forced himself to follow, not so much because he believed in the feasibility of what they were attempting, but only to avoid being left there alone. A dozen times in the next seconds he was sure that he could not retain his precarious grip. A dozen times he considered the possibility of merely letting go. It would be better to accept the inevitable, he thought. It would be better to admit defeat and be done with it. But something kept him going and, after what seemed an eternity, he looked up and saw that the top was actually within reach. Then a hand clutched his and he was pulled roughly over the edge to safety beyond it.

Paul gave him no time to rest there.

"*Niguim*, hurry—there's not much time."

Down the track Ken saw the lights of the caboose drawing near them. The train would be gone in an instant. Paul led the way to the end of the cut and then down to track level. Suddenly he turned sharply away.

"This way, Ken. Quickly. Follow me."

He led the way down a steep bank, over the broken rock that formed the ballast for the roadbed. At the bottom there was a drainage pipe, perhaps five feet in diameter, leading under the tracks. Paul released Ken's hand and, bending low at the waist, disappeared in the blackness of the pipe. Without enthusiasm, but too weary to resist, Ken followed.

The pipe seemed incredibly long. There was a little water in the bottom of it and the footing was treacherous. But at last they came out on the other side of the tracks. Then Paul led them away at right angles to the roadbed, straight into the forest. He dragged Ken on for several hundred yards before he allowed them a pause for rest.

They sank limply to the ground. Both listened carefully, but there was no sound of pursuit from behind them.

"I think we've done it," Paul said at last. "We've shaken them off. They didn't know about that pipe."

"Yeah, but how are we going to get to the station now? They'll be on the track between us and Kinniwabi."

"We don't have to use the track," Paul said. "I just realized something I should have thought of a long time ago."

"What's that?"

Paul pointed to his left.

"The creek is right over there a few feet—the one that comes into Kinniwabi just the other side of your place. Old Jim White Dog keeps a canoe near here somewhere to use on his trap line. I know I can find it. We'll go the rest of the way in comfort."

Paul walked almost straight to the canoe. It was pulled well up into the bushes, but he found it within minutes of reaching the stream. There were two old paddles under it and soon they were gliding down the narrow stream between the crowding muskeg banks. After the long, heartbreaking trek overland, paddling was almost effortless. In what seemed like no time at all, they saw a widening light in the sky ahead of them, indicating that the lake was near.

They came out into it a moment later and a short paddle along the shore took them to the Warren cottage.

There was an unmistakable brightness in the east, now, and dawn was clearly at hand. Already it was light enough to identify the outlines of the outboard motor crate still lying where Les Crowe and Dinnie Hackett had dropped it so long ago.

They went up to the cottage. In the living room the lamp, which could so easily have negated their plans, had burned dry, leaving a charred wick and a smoky chimney. The dish-towel Ken had used to dry his dinner dishes lay where he had thrown it across the back of a kitchen chair.

They drank several glasses of water each and rejected the idea of food as representing too much trouble, even though they were both hungry.

"What now?" asked Paul.

"I don't know about you, but I just have to see if we really got a picture of those two before I turn in," Ken answered. "I'm dying to go to bed but I'll never sleep any-way, until I know."

"Neither will I."

"I need electricity and running water to develop the pic-ture," Ken said. "Maybe Moose MacGregor's place would be the best bet."

"Now? At this hour?" Paul asked. "It's not even five thirty yet."

"I know, but if we've got what I think we've got on this roll, Moose won't mind being wakened. He'd do anything to clear John."

Paul helped to gather up the developing equipment and a few minutes later they were on their way. The sun was just edging up over the eastern tree line as they paddled in to the

155

dock at the station. The electric lights were still burning eerily on the dock and along the station platform. There was not a sound.

They walked along the tracks to the forest ranger's house. The dew was thick on the grass as they went up the path to his door.

"Well, here goes," Ken said, knocking lightly on the wood.

There was no response and he tapped harder.

"Who is it?" a sleepy voice called from inside.

"It's me, Ken Warren, and Paul Onaman," Ken answered.

"Okay—just a second."

A moment later the big forest ranger opened the door, yawning and running his fingers through his tousled hair.

"Fine time to be waking a man . . . good heavens, what the heck happened to you two?"

For the first time the boys realized how they must look. Their clothes were dirty and torn. Blood from innumerable scratches had run down their arms and hardened there. The faces still showed abundant trace of the mud they had rubbed on to ward off the mosquitoes back in the swamp. Their hair was matted and tangled.

"It's a long story, Moose," Ken told him, "and we'll give you all the details later. The main thing is the picture we have in this camera. If it turns out, it will show who the real robbers are and clear John and Henry."

"You've got a picture? How fast can you get it developed? When can we see it?"

"I've got the stuff here to develop it, if I can use your bathroom. I need darkness and running water."

"Sure, you can. And hurry, for pete's sake."

"Maybe Paul will fill you in on the story," Ken suggested, "while I'm doing this. I won't be long."

He went into the bathroom and closed the door. He closed off the small window with its curtains and some towels hanging on a rack over the sink. Then he switched off the light to satisfy himself that the room would be dark enough. With the light on again, he prepared his chemicals in the various trays and pans provided in his kit.

Then, switching off the light, he took the film from the camera. It was hard working in the pitch darkness but he would have to do his best. He put the film in a tray of developing fluid and left it for the length of time specified in his instructions. He waited impatiently for the minutes to tick away, timing it by the luminous hands on his wrist-watch. Finally the time was up and he transferred the film to the fixer. Again there was nothing to do but wait. The thought crossed his mind that the strip of black film near his hand might possibly be blank. Sometimes things did go wrong. What terrible irony it would be if all their efforts had been in vain! He forced the thought from his mind. No use worrying about that. They'd know soon enough now.

How long did he have to leave it in the fixer? He tried to remember the printed instructions. If only he weren't so tired. It needed sheer physical effort to make his mind focus on the job at hand. What had it said—a half hour, an hour? Think. Ten minutes, that's what it said—just ten minutes. He waited while the hands on his watch crawled around. Now.

He ran cold water from the tap over the black negative for a minute and then dried it gently with a towel. Now he

157

could let in a little light. He pulled the curtains back slightly from the window and held the negative up to the weak light.

There was something there, all right, but he couldn't make out any details, nor even get a vague idea of the quality of his picture.

He plugged in the printing box, put the negative and printing paper on the glass and closed the small door over it. Now, switch on the light inside the box and count. Don't spoil it by hurrying too much. One, two, three, four, five, six, seven, eight seconds—that's it.

His hand was trembling as he opened the small door, and then relief flooded over him. There was his picture. He took it out gingerly and held it towards the window. There was the boathouse in the background and the low bushes beside the dock. The light from the flash emphasized outlines of building, branches and trees, making sharp patterns of black and white. In the foreground were two figures, bent under the weight of the crated outboard motor. Both men were looking straight into the camera, drawn by the sudden flash in the darkness. There was surprise and fear in their faces, their eyes unnaturally wide, their mouths open. But the features were sharp and clear and identification would be beyond doubt. Oh, you beautiful picture, Ken thought, excitement driving the fatigue from his body.

He rinsed the print quickly in the necessary chemicals, dried it and then turned towards the door.

He held the picture up triumphantly as he stepped into the living room. Paul and Moose MacGregor turned, anxiety in their eyes.

"We got it! We got it!" Ken shouted. "It's all there as clear as day. Every loving detail."

The others crowded on either side of him.

"Boy," said Paul, "oh, boy."

"Happy day," the forest ranger added quietly. "You've got them dead to rights. With the evidence you two can give, I should think this will do the trick. I think it will do just fine."

He went into his bedroom and began to dress. The two boys went quietly into the other room and fell side by side across the bed. In an instant they were both fast asleep.

Doing up his shirt on the other side of the partition, Moose MacGregor added another comment.

"I think we should have John and Henry out inside of a day or two," he said. "Ought to be back here by the week-end for sure."

But there was no answer from the other room.

Chapter 18

Ken and Paul slept as though drugged. The sun crept slowly up into the sky, passed its zenith and began its long glide towards the western horizon. The noon train stopped at Kinniwabi and hurtled on towards the east. The railway section hands had come in on their jigger, had their lunch and gone back to work. Through all of this the boys' sleep was unbroken. When they finally wakened, early in the afternoon, most of the loose ends had been tied up.

Early that morning, just after they had fallen asleep, Moose MacGregor had walked down to the station. His insistent pounding had finally roused D. R. Morley. The station agent, disgruntled but immaculate in a paisley dressing gown, had not tried to conceal his irritation as he opened the door.

"Don't you realize what time it is? What are you pounding on the door for, at this hour?"

"I know what time it is," Moose had answered, "but I want to send a wire."

"Well, can't you wait till after breakfast?"

Moose had explained the urgency and his determination to have the police return that day.

"I don't want John and Henry to spend one hour more than necessary in that jail," he had said. "And the sooner that Les Crowe and Dinnie Hackett are there in their place, the happier I'll be. Your breakfast will keep for a few minutes. Let's get on with it."

The station agent had been far from overjoyed but had sent the wire. The news, which spread with amazing rapidity, had been received with varying reactions by other people at Kinniwabi. Mr. Simpson had learned of it with profound relief. Wilbur Crowe had accepted it with curses and sullen resentment. The cottagers heard it with detached interest. For them the sense of personal involvement had abated once the police had taken charge. Janet Morley had closed her eyes silently and a tear had run down her cheek. The Ojibway had gone about their morning chores, unaware of what had happened.

The two policemen who had arrested John and Henry arrived back at Kinniwabi on the noon train. They had talked to Moose MacGregor, inspected the picture and sent an urgent wire to their headquarters in the city. It was a long message, describing the picture and how it had been obtained. An hour later their answer had come back over the wire. They were to pick up Les Crowe and Dinnie Hackett. John Onaman and Henry Two Turtles were being released.

The arrest of Dinnie Hackett and Les Crowe was unspectacular and anticlimactic. A section hand, a friend of John Onaman's, had reported seeing two men sleeping in the bush a short distance east of the station. The two policemen had hitched a ride on the jigger and taken their quarry into custody without resistance. Their prisoners were handcuffed to a bench in the baggage room of the station by shortly after two o'clock that afternoon.

About that time Ken and Paul were taking the liberty of making themselves some breakfast in Moose MacGregor's kitchen. Their deep sleep had soothed away the fatigue of their arduous night, but on awakening they had both been weak from hunger.

"I could eat a bull moose—live," Ken said, as they sat down to bacon and eggs and toast.

"Me, too," Paul agreed, "and a couple of cows for good measure."

By the time they had satisfied their hunger, washed their dishes and strolled down to the station, it was all over. The two policemen had left for the city with their prisoners a half hour earlier in the caboose of a freight train. Ken and Paul were the center of attention around the station, but they recognized that most of the interest sprang from mere curiosity. Only the comments of Mr. Simpson made any real impression on Ken.

"That's the best thing that's happened around here in a long time," the old storekeeper said, speaking softly so that Paul would not overhear. "You'll never know how much it means to the Indians, just to know that somebody cares. It's more important than you know, Ken."

Still using Jim White Dog's canoe, Ken and Paul paddled over to the cottage. When they parted at the dock, Paul took a few strokes out into the lake and then turned, resting his paddle across the gunwales of the canoe.

"Ken," he said, "thanks."

Ken suddenly remembered that he had not told his friend the bad news about the Ojibway land, but did not have the heart to break it to him then. There would be time enough for that later.

"That's okay, Paul," he said. "We did it, eh?"

"Yes," said Paul. "We did it. We really did it."

There was more than the usual excitement at the train the next evening, for John Onaman and Henry Two Turtles arrived along with Ken's parents and Aunt Marion and the usual complement of weekend visitors. Ken sat up late back at the cottage, narrating the details of Wednesday night's adventure. There was occasional apprehension in the eyes of his parents as he described the trap and the long flight through the woods, but there was pride, too.

"I'll confess that I'm glad we didn't know what was going on that night," his father said when the story was finished, "but I guess we all owe you some congratulations."

His mother laughed quietly.

"I was going to tell you that I didn't want you ever to do it again," she said, smiling, "but I guess the chances of that are pretty slim. Good for you, Ken."

With John home, Ken had intended to tell Paul the bad news about Empirico the following day, but he just could not make himself do it. Instead he spent Saturday by himself. In the morning he cut wood for the stove and fireplace and after lunch he went to the head of the lake to fish. Trolling up and down beside the weed beds there, he kept one eye on the Indian village but did not see Paul. He caught three fairly small pickerel, enough for dinner, and then headed back toward the cottage. Even the fishing had failed to take his mind off the unpleasant chore facing him.

He didn't sleep well that night, and rose early. After a quick swim and a solitary breakfast, he took the canoe and went across the lake to the village. There were a few things he had to get at the station and he made up his mind to drop in and break the news to Paul on the way.

Paul was still elated about John's release and Ken had great difficulty making himself bring the conversation around to the unpleasant subject. At last he decided that he might as well go straight to the point. No amount of pre-amble was going to soften the blow.

"We got word from the lawyer about the land," he said. "You know, the lawyer in my dad's company."

Paul's eyes met his, but he did not reply.

"It isn't good, Paul," Ken said, and hurried on to tell his friend the details.

Paul did not say anything for a long time after he had finished speaking. He turned his eyes towards the ground and defeat seemed to fall again on his slight shoulders.

"That's that then, I guess," he muttered at last.

"I guess it is."

There was a long silence between them, a silence that went straight to Ken's heart. At last he felt compelled to break it.

"Come on down to the store with me," he said. "I've got to get a few things."

"No, not now," Paul said. "I don't feel like it now."

"I know you don't, but I need some company. Come on. It won't do any good to sit here."

"Before long I won't be able to sit here," Paul said, but he agreed to go along to the station.

They made the trip in silence and walked up to the station and across the track to the store with their heads slumped and eyes down. It was a sad contrast with their triumph of the previous days.

Ken gathered together the groceries his mother had requested and set them on the counter in front of Mr. Simpson.

"Anything else, Ken?" the storekeeper asked.

"No, that's all, I guess."

Mr. Simpson looked up at him from the bill he had started to make out.

164

"You two look pretty depressed after your great day Thursday," he said quietly. "What's the matter?"

"Just about everything," Ken said. "We heard from the lawyer in town and it looks like the Ojibway don't have a chance."

"Why is that?"

Ken told him the story. Putting the words together and forcing them through his lips required a real physical effort. He felt tired, dispirited, defeated.

The old storekeeper listened intently, asking an occasional question. When Ken had finished he stood thoughtfully for a moment behind the counter.

"This creek is the real key to the whole thing, then?"

"Yes," Ken said wearily, "the settlement will be based on the location of that creek. And there is only one creek, of course, and it's in the wrong place."

Mr. Simpson banged his fist lightly on the counter top several times, his lips pursed and his eyes narrowed in thought. Then he turned towards the door of their living quarters.

"Excuse me a second," he said. "I'll be right back."

He was gone for a long time and the boys had picked up the groceries and were on their way towards the door when he returned. There was a sparkle in his one active eye.

"Wait a minute," he said. "I wanted to check something to make sure. You're right about there being only one creek. There is only one creek—now. But it wasn't always that way."

Ken felt a quickening of excitement.

"What do you mean?" he asked.

"When I came here first—that was in '06—the water was

165

quite a bit higher. It dropped when they put in the dam at Blind Falls, just before the first World War. After that there was only one creek. But before that—there were *two* creeks."

Ken looked at Paul.

"What two creeks?" he asked.

"There was the same one there is now," the old store-keeper said, "and there was a second creek further up, on the other side of it. The other one came into those weed beds up at the head of the lake. It was a good size, too—big enough to have bass in it."

"Are you sure?"

"Of course, I'm sure. I paddled up it a hundred times. And what's more this old survey map proves it."

He spread the map out on the counter. It was frayed at the edges and split where it had been folded. The paper was yellowing and finger-marked, but the cartography was still clear.

"There it is," Mr. Simpson said, moving his finger across the map. "They used to call it Six Mile Creek—don't know why. You can see it there as plain as day."

There was no mistaking the twisting line on the old map. It came into Kinniwabi from the northwest, entering the lake a full quarter mile the other side of the Ojibway clearing. And just to the right of the undulating line which repre-sented the creek were the beautifully clear words "Indian Territory."

"That must be the creek referred to in the deed," said Mr. Simpson. "The deed says that Empirico's land runs east-wards to the creek. If they'd intended it to mean the other creek, the one that's there now, they surely would have made it clear that it was the second creek, and not the first, that they were talking about."

"Sure, they would have," said Ken, thoughtfully. "Is there any doubt about the accuracy of this map?"

"Shouldn't be," said Mr. Simpson. "It's an official government survey map. Look at the date—1903—the year before Empirico's deed and ten years before the water level was dropped."

"But why wouldn't the lawyer in the city know about this map?" Paul asked.

"I don't know," said the storekeeper, "but probably because it was never published. There were a lot of surveys made in those days for special purposes, but not many of them were printed in large quantities. I only happen to have this one because the surveyor was a friend of mine and he sent it to me."

"This should do it," Ken said in elation. "This should really do it. They can't argue with this evidence, can they?"

"I don't know much about the law," Mr. Simpson said, "but I sure know where that creek was. I can show you the bed to this day, back there in the woods."

They left the store then, and it seemed that a great weight had been lifted from their shoulders. The sun was dancing off the lake and it was summer again and there was beauty all around them.

"We're not beaten yet," Paul said as they parted.

"Not by a long shot," Ken said. "I'd think we have a really good chance, now."

He dropped Paul off at the village and hurried across the lake. It was lunchtime, but he made his family wait until he had related the news.

Mr. Warren was as enthusiastic as Ken about the importance of the discovery. In the afternoon he and Ken returned to the station to talk further with Mr. Simpson. When they left an hour later they took with them the old map and a signed statement from Mr. Simpson testifying that he had personally seen the second stream, had in fact traversed it many times, and knew from personal knowledge that the map was correct.

"If it'll help any, I'll be glad to go into the city and tell them myself," he said.

"I don't think you'll have to do that," Mr. Warren told him. "Your statement and his map should be all the proof they need. As you say, Empirico's deed would certainly have specified that it referred to the eastern stream if that was what was intended. The fact that it doesn't specifically say so makes it obvious that the reference was to the other stream—the one that no longer exists."

"That's sure the way it looks to me," said the storekeeper. "Now that I think about it, Six Mile Creek was always looked on as the boundary of the Indian land. I know that in the old days nobody would have dreamed of hunting on the east bank of that stream. I didn't follow it because I didn't want to trespass on the Indians' land."

When Mr. Warren left on the weekend train that evening, the map and Mr. Simpson's statement were in his briefcase. Ken watched the train pick up speed as it disappeared around the bend. He saw his father for a last instant waving at the window of one of the day coaches, and then the train was gone. The lights were on along the station platform as Ken went down to the boat. He remembered earlier in the summer when the Sunday evening train had departed for the city in full daylight. Lights were on in some of the cottages as he pushed away from the dock, underlining the fact that the summer was fast passing.

He pulled the starter cord on the motor, adjusted the throttle and turned the bow towards the point. A thin moon hung in the eastern sky. He zipped up his jacket against the early evening chill and thought with pleasure of the cottage across the lake, with its welcoming lights and the warming crackle in the fireplace.

Far up the lake, on the other side, he could see the lights of the Indian village and he wondered what Paul was doing at that moment.

He felt happy and confident and he remembered his father's last words, just before he had climbed the steps into the train.

"I'll talk to the lawyer first thing in the morning," he had said. "This new evidence should throw a different light on the whole business. I don't see how we can lose now, but we should know by next weekend. I'll see you on Friday, Ken. Till then, keep your fingers crossed."

Ken smiled to himself there in the wan light of the new moon and silently crossed the first two fingers on his free right hand. Then, just for added luck, he crossed his ankles as well.

Chapter 19

Then it was the beginning of the last week of summer. It came to Ken suddenly that Monday morning, as he walked down to the dock for a pre-breakfast swim. Seven more days and it would all be over. One week before Labor Day, and then it would be back to the city, back to school, back to work.

The changes were subtle. It was still hot and the bright sun still shimmered across the water. The cicadas were busy as always. The bass and sunfish darted away from the dock as they did every morning. But, once you thought about it, you realized that the slant of the sun was more oblique than it had been earlier in the summer. The dew was heavier on the grass of the path. It was a little cooler in the shadows under the trees.

There were other signs of the summer's passing. The blueberry bushes were drying. The frail early flowers had given way to the blossoms of full summer. The chokecherries and the pin cherries were ripening. In the wild rice beds along the far margin of the lake the heads of grain would soon be ready for the harvest. The poplar trees showed an occasional touch of yellow and on the point of the island a single maple tree provided a flash of early fire against the green of the willows.

A family of young partridges, mere balls of uneven feathers in the early days of July, no longer scurried through the tall grass behind the cottage under the frantic protection of

170

their mother. They flew now, in the strength of their near maturity, and burst into the air with pounding wings if anyone stumbled upon them. The bass had grown lethargic in their feeding and the pickerel had moved into deep water. Some of the early migrating birds were already beginning to flock.

The realization saddened Ken. Summer was always like that. For a long time each year it seemed as if the warm, rich days stretched infinitely into the future, full and unchanging and impregnable. And then, suddenly, you saw a changing leaf or a formation of ducks against the morning sky and you knew that the best part of it was over.

Never mind, he thought as he climbed from the water onto the warm boards of the dock, there's still a week left. One more week—time to do lots of things. Seven final days to be enjoyed to the hilt, the more precious because they were few. And with any luck now, because of Mr. Simpson's evidence, the summer would end on a much happier note than he had envisaged a few days earlier.

He and Paul spent almost all of the final week together. They explored new canoe routes and new trails. They revisited many of the places they had discovered earlier. They fished their secret trout stream again, and paddled and portaged once more to their favorite island in Cygnet Lake.

"I wish you were going to be here in the fall," Paul said, one morning towards the end of the week. That's the best time."

"I do, too," said Ken, "but what's so special about the fall?"

"There's so much to do. That's when we bring in the wild rice. That's hard work, but it's fun. You get the biggest pike in the fall, too. I've caught pike here in October so big you'd hardly believe it."

171

"What about the pickerel?"

"No, they don't bite very well then. Neither do the bass. But the pike get hungrier as it gets colder. We could go down to Cygnet and . . ."

He stopped with the realization that he was beginning to plan something which would not happen.

"I'd sure like that," Ken said, "if there was some way to do it."

"There's the hunting, too," Paul said. "Partridge and ducks. Always lots to eat in the fall."

They fell silent, full of the summer's ending.

"There's Thanksgiving," Ken said with a sudden flash of hope. "Early in October—we get the Monday off at school. How would that be for hunting?"

"Just right," Paul said, "but what are you thinking?"

"Oh, I was just fooling around with an idea. I wonder if my dad might let me come back down for that holiday weekend."

"You could come down on the late train Friday night," Paul said. "There's no special then, but the transcontinental gets here about eleven o'clock."

"And I could go back on the early morning train Monday morning—or, better still, Tuesday morning. I'd only miss a half-day of school."

"We could shoot partridge and ducks and go fishing and . . ."

"We'd better not get too excited," Ken said. "I don't know whether he'd let me do it or not. They'd have to leave the cottage open and the boat in the water."

"We could close up your cottage between us," Paul said, "and put the boat away. Then I could take you over to meet the train when you had to leave."

The magic of the idea gripped them both.

"Do you think there's a chance?" Paul asked.

"I just don't know. But there's no harm in giving it a try. I'll tackle my dad when he gets down on Friday night."

Thus the question of a possible Thanksgiving weekend was added to a deeper concern for the news that Mr. Warren would bring about the Ojibway land. They did not talk about this problem during that final week, but it was constantly in the back of their minds. If only the lawyer was as impressed as they were with Mr. Simpson's new evidence!

When Friday evening came, Ken was the first to arrive at the station to meet the train. He passed Mr. Morley on the platform, but the station agent did not return his greeting. He had been unfriendly to Ken ever since the arrest of Les Crowe and Dinnie Hackett and the release of the two young Ojibways. Ken did not particularly care, but he wondered at the bitterness that would lead to such unfriendliness. In any case the station agent's hostility was more than compensated for by the warm smile Ken received from his daughter, Janet.

He talked to Mr. Simpson for a while and then returned across the track to wait for the train's arrival. The blackboard on the platform wall announced that it was running on time and a moment later Ken heard it whistle around the long bend at the far side of the lake.

The sun was low in the west and the train lights were on as it ground to a stop beside the station.

Ken watched along the line of coaches as the Kinniwabi passengers began to disembark. His father was one of the first to step down and Ken hurried to meet him. As they came together, Ken searched his father's eyes for a clue to the news he might bring.

Mr. Warren looked steadily at his son and then smiled. "I think it's going to be all right," he said. "The lawyer says that the new evidence should change everything. He says it should be okay, now."

Ken felt a great wave of relief pass over him.

"Really?" he asked. "Does it really look like we'll win?"

"Let's go down to the boat," his father said. "I'll tell you all about it when we get to the cottage, but it does look as though we'll win. The lawyer said to tell you that he's sure the Ojibway will be able to stay where they are."

They crossed the lake in the stillness of late twilight. As the sun went down the light breeze took on a cool edge and by the time they reached the cottage they were glad of the warmth from the fireplace. It was almost full dark by the time Mr. Warren had his dinner, and the light from the lamps and the cherry crackle of the flames in the fireplace were welcome protection against the night.

Mr. Warren described in detail his discussion with the company lawyer. The old map and the sworn statement from Mr. Simpson had completely changed the situation. The whole case had always rested on the actual location of the creek dividing Empirico's purchase from the Ojibway land. Until the previous weekend the judgment could only have gone to the company. The new facts made it just as sure, he felt, that any court would find in favor of the Indians. In property cases, he said, you could never be certain, but he thought that confidence was abundantly justified under the new circumstances.

"That's wonderful," Mrs. Warren said. "I'm so glad for you, Ken, and for Paul."

"I don't know what difference it makes," Aunt Marion said. "They'll probably drift off somewhere else in a few months anyway. I'm amazed at you, wasting the lawyer's time."

"Marion," Mr. Warren said, and his carefully controlled voice showed that he was angry for one of the few times Ken could remember, "why do you insist on expressing your prejudices? Whatever you may think about the Indians is your business, but you must surely have some regard for law and justice. We're simply trying to prevent a wrong being done—and, thanks to Mr. Simpson, it looks as if we might succeed."

Aunt Marion put down her book and stalked out of the room, her head high and her lips set.

"I'm sorry," Mr. Warren said to his wife. "I shouldn't have lost my temper, but she pushed me too far."

"Don't be sorry, dear," Ken's mother answered. "She had it coming and if you hadn't told her off, I would have. I'm just glad that it's going to work out."

"There's something else I wanted to ask you," Ken said, deciding to press his luck. "I was wondering if I could come down to Kinniwabi for Thanksgiving."

He went on to explain, telling them of his conversation with Paul and of the fun they could have on that weekend.

"We'd close up the cottage, put away the boat and look after all those things," he concluded.

"How would you get down?" his mother asked.

"I thought I could take the regular train on Friday night and go in early on Monday morning."

"You might as well stay over until Tuesday morning if you come down," his father said. "That would give you a full extra day and you'd only have to miss one morning of school."

175

"Come to think of it, that's right," Ken said, smiling happily to himself.

"What about the hunting?" his mother asked. "I don't much like the idea of guns. They always frighten me."

"You'd have to promise to be very careful," Mr. Warren said, "but I guess you'd be in good hands with Paul. I might be able to borrow a shotgun for you from one of the fellows at work."

There was some further discussion about arrangements, but in the end it was settled. Ken could come down on that Friday night and have three full days with Paul. They would leave the motorboat over at the station when they went in on Labor Day, asking Mr. Simpson to keep an eye on it in the meantime. Ken could bring some food down with him from the city and get what else he needed at the station store. He would have to put on the shutters and close up for the winter, but with Paul's help that would not be a problem.

"All right, then," Mr. Warren said, "you can have your weekend. I'm envious—wouldn't mind getting in a little partridge hunting, myself."

"Why don't you come, too?" Ken asked.

"No, no, this is your weekend, yours and Paul's. But you might bring us back a couple of birds for a Sunday dinner."

Ken could hardly wait to tell Paul. Right after breakfast in the morning he paddled across the lake to the village. It was an overcast morning with a threat of thunderstorms, but for Ken the sun was shining brightly.

First he told his friend of the good news from the lawyer. As he talked relief and joy made subtle changes in Paul's face. His friend's eyes grew gradually a little brighter and a faint smile appeared at the corners of his lips. These were changes that would not have been apparent to most people, and would not have been apparent to Ken a few weeks earlier, but he recognized them now.

As he finished, his friend nodded.

"That is good," he said quietly. "That is very good news."

"Wait a minute," Ken said. "There's more to come." And he told Paul about the Thanksgiving weekend.

"No kidding?" Paul asked. "You really can come?"

"Yes, I can come, and stay over until Tuesday morning, too. Won't we have a good time, eh?"

They talked for some time about their plans for Thanksgiving. They would go down to Cygnet Lake for one of the days, where the biggest pike lurked in the weed beds. There would be ducks there also, toward the end of the day.

"And we can pick up the odd partridge on the portages," Paul said.

Ken would leave his fishing tackle at the cottage and would bring down a shotgun and ammunition. They could both stay at the Warren cottage. Paul would make sure that there was lots of wood on hand and Ken would be responsible for their food supplies. They agreed that Ken would spend the first night at the cottage alone, with Paul coming over on Saturday morning.

"That train is often late," Ken said, "and there's no point in your having to hang around the station at that time of night."

Ken did not mind so much now that the summer was ending. Kinniwabi would be a different place in October, a place he had not so far known, and he was excited by the prospect. The remainder of that last weekend sped by quickly.

Although the cottage was not to be finally closed up, there was still plenty to be done before the family left for the city, and he was kept busy.

Late Monday afternoon he had a final swim and then got dressed, ready to go to the train. His city clothes felt strange and uncomfortable, especially the shoes after the long summer of wearing sneakers. He smiled to himself as he looked in the mirror of his room. His deep tan was accentuated by his white T-shirt. One of the first things I'll have to do, he thought, is get a haircut. I look as if I'd been in the bush for a year, instead of a couple of months.

They had their dinner, washed and put away the dishes for the last time that summer, and then started out for the station. The platform was crowded and this time almost everyone would become a passenger when the train arrived.

Paul met them on the platform and a moment later John Onaman stopped beside them.

"Thanks again, Ken," he said. "Thanks a lot."

Ken and Paul strolled along the track away from the crowd. The train, laboring under its extra end-of-summer load, was a little late, but then they heard it whistle a few miles down the track.

Ken looked out across the still water of the lake for a moment.

"Well," he said, "I guess I'd better get my bag and be ready to jump on the train."

"Yeah, but you'll be back before long."

They could see the headlight of the engine through the trees lining the long curve to the east.

"Sure I will," Ken said, "but I guess it's so long for now."

They walked back towards the crowd of people which was moving now towards the front of the platform.

178

"By the way," Ken asked, "how do you say good-bye in Ojibway?"

"We don't say it," Paul answered. He thought for a moment. "We say *B'jou* when we meet somebody, and the same thing when we leave them. But in Ojibway there is no word for good-bye."

"Well, then, we'll just say so long for now," Ken said.

"Yes," Paul said quietly, "so long—until Thanksgiving."

The train ground to a stop and Ken moved forward with the crowd until he could step into the day coach. As he walked along the aisle looking for his parents, the train began to move slowly ahead. He leaned down a little and looked out the window. The platform was sliding past as the train gradually gained momentum.

He saw Paul standing beside a baggage cart, searching the windows of the train. For an instant their eyes met. Ken waved and saw his friend's hand raised in return.

Then the station was gone. Ken caught one final glimpse of the lake through the long row of poplars along Gibson's Point. Then the train whistled as it plunged into the rock cut at the far end of the long curve and Kinniwabi was behind them.

Chapter 20

September was a busy month for Ken. First of all, of course, there was the return to school and the inevitable increase in the amount of homework he had to do. There were new teachers to adjust to, new subjects to deal with, a new timetable to learn. And there were old friendships to renew and new ones to begin. And there was football. Ken went out for the junior team at school and practices took up most of the time he had left over from studying.

In a surprisingly short time he found himself completely adjusted again to city life. Yet Kinniwabi was never far from his mind. He would be studying a book in his room when suddenly a picture of the lake, the harvest moon bright across the water, would come into his mind. Or he would see someone on the street or in the halls of the high school and remember Paul walking beside him along the railway track at the lake.

The lawyer at Mr. Warren's office had passed the map and Mr. Simpson's affidavit along to the authorities for their consideration in the matter of the Ojibway versus Empirico. He had done his part and the rest would be up to the parties more immediately concerned. What remained would be mere routine, now that the evidence was so clear-cut.

One evening as he walked home after football practice, Ken looked up to see a long, ragged V of wild geese against the pale and fading blue of the autumn twilight, and he realized that September was past. In a little more than a week he would be returning to Kinniwabi. One night his father brought home a shotgun he had borrowed from a man at the office. It was a single-barrel .410 which seemed almost to have been made for Ken. He loved the balance of it and the way it felt in his hands.

Then it was time to make preparations for the Thanksgiving weekend. He made a trip downtown on the preceding Saturday, got a hunting license at a sporting goods store and bought two boxes of shotgun shells. He made arrangements for an order of food to be delivered to the station so that it would go down on the same Friday night train that he was taking. He went to the railway station and bought his return ticket. He picked up some extra pairs of warm woolen socks, a new red hunting shirt. Then, on an impulse, he went around to the museum and, after considerable searching, found the pipe he had rescued from Lake of the Clouds that summer. He stood looking down at the case and remembered the hot day he had found it—his birthday. Once more he had that feeling of timeless, intimate liaison with its original owner. And he thought about Paul and the Ojibway and their deep roots, intertwined with his own. He enjoyed that day, but Kinniwabi was still a week away.

And then suddenly, miraculously, it was the Friday of the long October weekend. Ken got through school that day in a semi daze. He took notes, answered questions, worked at problems, but his mind was somewhere else. That night he would be on the way to Kinniwabi!

At last the final bell of the day rang and he took the bus to his house. He had dinner with his parents, listened to their last-minute instructions, and then it was time to go to the station.

"You're sure you don't want your father to drive you down?" his mother asked.

"No," said his father, firmly, "he can take a cab just as well. This is Ken's trip and anyway there's a television program that I want to watch."

Ken called the station and found that the train was running about an hour late. It's good, he thought, that Paul won't be waiting for me. Then he phoned a taxi company and ordered a cab to pick him up in time for the delayed departure of his train.

It seemed funny sitting there in the living room of his house and trying to realize that in a few hours he would be back at the cottage at Kinniwabi.

At last the doorbell sounded and his cab was there. Ken said good-bye to his parents, pacified his mother's eleventh hour doubts, and carried his baggage out to the waiting taxi. On the way to the station he looked at the street lights and the neon signs of the city and thought of the entirely different world to which he was returning. Just think, tomorrow morning he would stand on the dock and watch Paul come around the point!

The station was crowded with people departing to various points for the weekend. Ken sat on a bench, his baggage around him, and waited impatiently for departure time. Finally, they announced his train.

"Train number five," the loud speaker called, "the Federalist, now loading on track number three. Train number five, for all points east, will be departing in ten minutes. All aboard, please."

Ken picked up his baggage and went through the station rotunda to the lower level, from which the trains departed. He found the right line up and filed past the conductor, hanging onto his baggage with some difficulty while he showed his ticket. Then it was up the steps to the track level.

"Where to, son?" the trainman asked him.

"Kinniwabi," Ken answered.

"That way—third car back," the trainman told him.

Ken found a seat by the window in the lighted day coach. The train was already crowded. There was a great assortment of people. Businessmen on their way home from meetings in the city. Women with small children. Secretaries returning to spend the long weekend with their families in northern hometowns. And here and there, scattered throughout the car, were men who Ken knew belonged in the bush. You could tell them by their rough clothes and by their different bearing. That huge man there with the beard —was he a prospector, perhaps? And the two younger men in the bush jackets—were they employees of some lumber company, or government officials? Maybe they work for Empirico, Ken thought. Well, if so, they could forget about taking the Ojibway land at Kinniwabi. At the far end of the car there was a young Indian couple with three small children. They sat quietly, almost listlessly. The children laughed and played as did the other children in the car, but the young man and young woman sat silently. They are out of their element here, Ken thought.

Then they were moving out of the station. Ken watched through the window. The train moved slowly past city streets where red-lighted barriers blocked the way for impatient automobiles and warning bells rang. He saw his father's office building and, far uptown, the outline of the city's biggest department store. Out in the suburbs they passed a football game being played under the lights of a high school stadium. And then the geometric formalities of the city gradually petered out and the train was moving through the blackness of the country, punctuated only by the lights of increasingly isolated farmhouses.

For a while Ken read his magazine. He bought a chocolate bar and a soft drink from the vendor and enjoyed a feeling of luxurious well-being as he relaxed in the warm comfort of the modern day coach.

The train sped on its way, its headlight cutting a swath through the darkness, its whistle screaming a warning to anything that might venture into its path. One by one, the stations fell behind them—Swanson, Howard's Falls, Hall's Glen, Alma, Cedar Rapids, Moose Lake. And then, suddenly, the conductor came through the car calling "Piney Rapids" and Ken realized that Kinniwabi was only a few minutes away. He gathered his belongings from the rack over his head and from under the seat, and sat waiting for the conductor's call.

It was pitch dark outside the window of the train. The light from the windows illuminated only to the edge of the roadbed and beyond that the endless bush stretched away into the blackness.

"Kinniwabi, Kinniwabi," the conductor called at last. "This way out." Ken got to his feet as the train began to slow. We're going around that long bend behind Gibson's Point, he thought, as he started towards the exit. He caught a glimpse of the station lights and then the train had stopped and the conductor was placing the portable step beside the car door.

"Don't shoot too many ducks," the trainman said, and then Ken stepped out onto the platform at Kinniwabi. Almost as soon as his feet touched the ground, the train was moving on again, seemingly impatient at this insignificant interruption in its headlong rush through the night.

Apart from the platform lights, there was no sign of life. The store across the track was in darkness. So was the station agent's living quarters and Moose MacGregor's house farther along.

Ken arranged his luggage so that he could carry it in one trip, and headed down the path towards the lake. The station lights threw some illumination as far as the end of the dock, but beyond that was only unbroken darkness. The motorboat swung gently beside the dock where they had left it.

In many ways it was like a summer night. Bugs darted chaotically around the bare bulbs of the dock lights. The sounds of the lake were generally as they might have been in August. Light waves lapped beneath his feet. A fish jumped out from the dock. At first it seemed warm.

Ken peeled the cover from the boat, loaded his luggage and stepped into the stern. There was enough gas in the motor to make the trip to the cottage, and after a few preliminary pulls the ignition caught and he started away from the dock. It was dark and lonely on the lake, but the stars were bright above and almost as bright as they reflected in the water. He could not make out a tree line, but guessed at the location of the point and hit it right on the nose. By then he had become aware of the nip in the air. There was almost no wind and the chill did not hit him suddenly. Instead it was a subtle thing, coming over him gradually, penetrating his clothing and making him draw further into his parka.

He was glad when the boat drifted to a stop beside the cottage dock. He took a flashlight from his bag and went up the path, noticing the unfamiliar carpet of brown leaves under his feet. A moment later he had the cottage open and lamps burning in the kitchen and living room. He would put some of the groceries away before he turned in, but first a brisk blaze in the fireplace was in order, to take away the chill.

He piled a newspaper and kindling on the grate and a minute later the crackle of flames filled the room. It seemed strange but good to be back at the cottage. On a shelf next to the fireplace he noticed a book Aunt Marion had read during the summer. There was his mother's sewing basket where she had left it by the big green chair. The transition from city to cottage had been so abrupt that he felt an almost unprecedented sense of exhilaration. In the morning, the very next morning, Paul would be there!

On second thought, maybe he would put off straightening things up until morning. He felt suddenly sleepy and the thought of nestling under a warm eiderdown was too appealing to postpone. He put a couple of big logs on the fire, carried a lamp into his bedroom, and quickly crawled in between the sheets.

He slept soundly, waking only once in the middle of the night, just long enough to add one more blanket to the pile on his bed. The fire was out by then and he considered relighting it, but the chill on the air sent him hurrying back to bed.

It was morning when he next wakened. His room was cold, but a bright sun through his window gave promise of a good day. He lay there for a few minutes enjoying the sensation and then, realizing that Paul would soon be there, he jumped out of bed and dressed quickly. He went into the kitchen, shivering slightly, and got a good fire started in the box stove. Now to get some water boiling for hot porridge.

He took the water pail from beside the door and started down the path to the dock. As he had noticed the previous night, a lot of leaves were already down. Those that remained were past their peak of brilliance and beginning to fade to russet brown.

He walked out on the dock, breathing deeply. There was a clean, invigorating freshness to the air that made his blood tingle. Oh, it was great to be back!

He stood at the end of the dock and looked out over the lake. They would probably go fishing up there at the head of the lake before the weekend was over, and hunt for partridge on the island, and shoot ducks there by the creek. They would . . .

Suddenly his eyes stopped and a chill ran along his spine. The Indian clearing. The tents were gone. No boats were pulled up on the beach in the foreground. No smoke curled up in the morning air. No dogs barked against the stillness. The village looked empty, lifeless, deserted. The strength seemed to drain from Ken's body. He stood there not believing what he saw. It couldn't be. It just could not be. He stood there, unmoving.

At last he jerked free the tie ropes and got into the boat. His chilled fingers fumbled with the choke and the gas tap. Frantically he yanked the starting cord.

The motor caught on the first pull and the sound of it was almost indecently loud in the tranquil morning. He opened it up wide and headed across the lake. As he neared the beach he could see that the village had indeed been evacuated. The roofs on two of the dwellings were caved in. The door on another hung ajar. Windows were broken. A ghostly silence hung over the clearing.

He knew that there was no point in landing. The Ojibway

were gone. He slowed the motor for a minute and then threw the throttle over again and headed towards the station.

Mr. Simpson was behind the counter in his store, weighing brown sugar from a hundred-pound sack into brown paper bags.

"Well, Ken," he said, looking up, "it's good to—"

"What happened to the Ojibway, Mr. Simpson?" Ken asked in a low voice. "What happened to Paul and the others?"

The old man looked into Ken's eyes for a long moment and then returned to his sugar and scales. For several seconds he did not answer.

"Gone," he said at last.

"Gone where?" Ken asked, his voice rising. "Where have they gone, and why?"

Again the old man was slow in answering.

"Just gone," he added finally. "Gone north somewhere. Don't know where. Gone two weeks now, right after they brought in the rice crop. I don't know who'll bring it in next year. Maybe nobody."

"But I thought it was all fixed," Ken said is disbelief. "I was sure we'd win the case. I was sure they'd be able to stay."

Mr. Simpson shook his head slowly and a sad smile came over his thin lips.

"No," he said haltingly, "not fixed. I guess you don't fix a thing like that, not with a company like Empirico. Not a company lawyer and a few Indians and a young boy like you and an old storekeeper like me. They're too big. Got so many lawyers working for them that they'd be bound to find a way."

"But what about the other creek? What about your evidence?"

"Not good enough, Ken, I guess," said the old man.

"But . . . I just can't believe it."

"I'm sure what they did was legal," Mr. Simpson added. "They must have found something we didn't know about. Everybody is equal before the law—but, with all their lawyers, they were just a little more equal than we were, I guess."

"Maybe they could appeal," Ken said. "Maybe if—"

"No, Ken, not a chance. The Ojibway are proud. They're gone from here for good."

"But how do you know that for sure?"

"Because I know them. They won't come back now, no matter what happens."

Ken walked to the door and stood looking past the station to the lake.

"Don't feel too bad about it," the storekeeper said. "You did your best. Some things we can do, and some things we can't do."

Ken stood there silently for a long moment. He felt stunned, shocked, empty. A heavy veil of apathy had descended upon him. Resentment fought against a sense of helplessness, and loss.

"There's a train in to the city late this afternoon, isn't there?" he asked at last.

"Yes, there's a local—goes through here about four o'clock."

"I guess I'll go over and close up the cottage then, and catch that train. I can't put the boat away by myself, so if I left it here could you get somebody to look after it for the winter?"

"Sure, Ken, I'll look after that."

"Then I guess I'll be going."

He started to open the door and then turned back. "Did Paul give you any message for me before he left?" Mr. Simpson knotted string around a one-pound bag of sugar. "No, Ken, he didn't say anything. None of them came near the store. One morning they were just gone."

"When you see him will you tell him I was asking for him? I know he didn't want to come here this weekend because of how I'd feel. But find out where they are, will you, Mr. Simpson? And tell him I'll look him up next summer."

The old man nodded.

"Yes, I'll do that Ken."

He went out then and walked slowly past the station and on down toward the lake. It looked suddenly bleak and empty and Ken had little heart for crossing it.

He would be glad when the afternoon train arrived. He hoped it would be on time.

The Author

John Craig is the author of several entertaining and unusual books for younger readers, including *Wagons West* and *The Long Return,* which have been published in several countries. Adults have enjoyed his provocative suspense novel *In Council Rooms Apart* and *The Pro,* a powerful story about professional hockey.

Mr. Craig has spent many summers in northwestern Ontario, the country that provides the setting for *No Word for Good-bye.* Mr. Craig has also written for and assisted in the production of the Canadian TV series *Rainbow Country,* set on Manitoulin Island.

When he isn't traveling in the wilderness he loves, John Craig lives in Toronto, Canada, with his wife and three children.